S0-AZB-308

# CARTRIDGE COUNTDOWN

Skye nearly wrenched the girl, Lida, off her feet when he broke into a run, glancing every which way at converging Paiutes. He was hopelessly outnumbered and he had only three bullets left.

A burly brave sprang from behind, a knife in his right hand. A stinging pang lanced Skye's left arm, and he fired point blank in the warrior's face.

Then he spotted two lean youths coming from the west. Both held bows, and Skye whipped his head back as an arrow went past him, its feathers brushing the tip of his nose. Skye lifted the Colt and squeezed off his next-to-last shot.

One slug left, thought Skye, and braves swarming after him . . . which added up to his chances being zero to none. . . .

## ∅ SIGNET

(0451)

# BLAZING NEW TRAILS
# WITH THE ACTION-PACKED
# TRAILSMAN SERIES
# BY JON SHARPE

| | | |
|---|---|---|
| ☐ | THE TRAILSMAN #114: THE TAMARIND TRAIL | (169794—$3.50) |
| ☐ | THE TRAILSMAN #115: GOLD MINE MADNESS | (169964—$3.50) |
| ☐ | THE TRAILSMAN #116: KANSAS KILL | (170237—$3.50) |
| ☐ | THE TRAILSMAN #117: GUN VALLEY | (170482—$3.50) |
| ☐ | THE TRAILSMAN #118: ARIZONA SLAUGHTER | (170679—$3.50) |
| ☐ | THE TRAILSMAN #119: RENEGADE RIFLES | (170938—$3.50) |
| ☐ | THE TRAILSMAN #120: WYOMING MANHUNT | (171063—$3.50) |
| ☐ | THE TRAILSMAN #121: REDWOOD REVENGE | (171306—$3.50) |
| ☐ | THE TRAILSMAN #122: GOLD FEVER | (171756—$3.50) |
| ☐ | THE TRAILSMAN #123: DESERT DEATH | (171993—$3.50) |
| ☐ | THE TRAILSMAN #124: COLORADO QUARRY | (172132—$3.50) |
| ☐ | THE TRAILSMAN #125: BLOOD PRAIRIE | (172388—$3.50) |
| ☐ | THE TRAILSMAN #126: COINS OF DEATH | (172604—$3.50) |
| ☐ | THE TRAILSMAN #127: NEVADA WARPATH | (173031—$3.50) |
| ☐ | THE TRAILSMAN #128: SNAKE RIVER BUTCHER | (173686—$3.50) |

Buy them at your local bookstore or use this convenient coupon for ordering.

**NEW AMERICAN LIBRARY**
**P.O. Box 999, Bergenfield, New Jersey 07621**

Please send me the books I have checked above.
I am enclosing $_____ (please add $2.00 to cover postage and handling).
Send check or money order (no cash or C.O.D.'s) or charge by Mastercard or
VISA (with a $15.00 minimum). Prices and numbers are subject to change without
notice.

Card #_____ Exp. Date _____
Signature_____
Name_____
Address_____
City _____ State _____ Zip Code _____

For faster service when ordering by credit card call **1-800-253-6476**

Allow a minimum of 4-6 weeks for delivery. This offer is subject to change without notice.

# THE
# TRAILSMAN
## 127

# NEVADA
# WARPATH

by

## Jon Sharpe

A SIGNET BOOK

SIGNET
Published by the Penguin Group
Penguin Books USA Inc., 375 Hudson Street,
New York, New York 10014, U.S.A.
Penguin Books Ltd, 27 Wrights Lane,
London W8 5TZ, England
Penguin Books Australia Ltd, Ringwood,
Victoria, Australia
Penguin Books Canada Ltd, 10 Alcorn Avenue,
Toronto, Ontario M4V 3B2
Penguin Books (N.Z.) Ltd, 182-190 Wairau Road,
Auckland 10, New Zealand

Penguin Books Ltd, Registered Offices:
Harmondsworth, Middlesex, England

First published by Signet,
an imprint of New American Library,
a division of Penguin Books USA Inc.

First Printing, July, 1992
10  9  8  7  6  5  4  3  2  1

Copyright © Jon Sharpe, 1992
All rights reserved

The first chapter of this book previously appeared in *Coins of Death,* the one
hundred twenty-sixth volume in this series.

 REGISTERED TRADEMARK—MARCA REGISTRADA

Printed in the United States of America

Without limiting the rights under copyright reserved above, no part of this
publication may be reproduced, stored in or introduced into a retrieval system, or transmitted, in any form, or by any means (electronic, mechanical,
photocopying, recording, or otherwise), without the prior written permission
of both the copyright owner and the above publisher of this book.

BOOKS ARE AVAILABLE AT QUANTITY DISCOUNTS WHEN USED TO PROMOTE
PRODUCTS OR SERVICES. FOR INFORMATION PLEASE WRITE TO PREMIUM MAR-
KETING DIVISION, PENGUIN BOOKS USA INC., 375 HUDSON STREET, NEW YORK,
NEW YORK 10014.

If you purchased this book without a cover you should be aware that this
book is stolen property. It was reported as "unsold and destroyed" to the
publisher and neither the author nor the publisher has received any payment
for this "stripped book."

# The Trailsman

Beginnings . . . they bend the tree and they mark the man. Skye Fargo was born when he was eighteen. Terror was his midwife, vengeance his first cry. Killing spawned Skye Fargo, ruthless, cold-blooded murder. Out of the acrid smoke of gunpowder still hanging in the air, he rose, cried out a promise never forgotten.

The Trailsman they began to call him all across the West: searcher, scout, hunter, the man who could see where others only looked, his skills for hire but not his soul, the man who lived each day to the fullest, yet trailed each tomorrow. Skye Fargo, the Trailsman, the seeker who could take the wildness of a land and the wanting of a woman and make them his own.

*1860 . . . Utah Territory, where mutual hatred spilled over into the bloody Paiute War, and not even the Pony Express could get through.*

# 1

The big man astride the splendid pinto stallion reined up in alarm and stared at the smoke rising skyward to the south. His lake blue eyes narrowed as he deciphered the message. Smoke signals were much like Morse code and were used to relay a wide variety of information. In this case, the warrior doing the signaling was telling the other members of his tribe that a lone white man was riding due west. Clearly, the warrior hoped his tribesmen would stop the rider.

Skye Fargo relaxed slightly. Since he was heading southwest, the smoke did not apply to him. But it meant another man was in trouble, or soon would be, and might need some help. Without hesitation he spurred the Ovaro into a gallop and rode hard toward the low, narrow ridge from which the smoke arose. The rider would be visible from up there, and he could decide whether to go to the man's aid or not.

He crossed an alkali flat to reach the ridge, using the mesquite and scraggly pines for cover as much as possible. The gradual slope was barren and he went up it in a rush, drawing his Colt as he neared the rim. He reached the top exactly where he wanted to be—as close to the source of the signal as possible. Which turned out to be within twenty yards of a lone brave on his knees beside a small fire, a damp blanket clutched in his hands.

From the Indian's near naked appearance and shaggy hair, Fargo recognized at a glance that the man was a Paiute. Back in Salt Lake City he'd been warned the Paiutes were on the warpath, and a friendly bartender had advised him to put off traveling to California until after the hostilities ended. But Fargo had pressed on, preferring to rely on the skills he had honed during his

9

life on the frontier to keep him out of trouble rather than wait weeks or even months until the Paiutes were defeated.

The brave took one look at the big man in buckskins and let the blanket fall onto the fire. Twisting, he grabbed a bow lying next to his left leg and notched an arrow to the string in a smooth motion. The barbed tip swung up and around and he began to draw back on the string.

Fargo fired, a single shot that struck the Paiute squarely in the center of the forehead and knocked him onto his back, his arms outflung. Stopping near the fire, Fargo noticed the smoldering blanket, then raised his gaze to scan the country beyond the ridge. Right away he saw the other rider, a figure in buckskins about half a mile distant who was galloping hell-bent for leather toward a wash. And well he should, because in blood-thirsty pursuit were five Paiutes on their lean war ponies.

Holstering his Colt, Skye moved to the southern edge and anxiously watched the grim tableau unfolding below. He was too far off to be of any help, and from the look of things the other man was going to escape unscathed. Already the lean figure enjoyed a commanding lead and his sturdy mount gained ground with every stride.

Suddenly, just as the rider was almost to the wash, his horse buckled and went down. The man leaped clear over his animal's head, stumbled, and fell to his knees. Then, rising, he drew a pistol and pivoted to face the charging warriors.

"Damn," Fargo muttered, and went down the ridge in a swirling cloud of dust. Angling toward the rider, he slipped his big Sharps from its scabbard and held it in his right hand. The intervening brush prevented him from observing the fight. He heard shots and whoops and hoped the man could hold out until he got there.

When still over two hundred yards away Fargo skirted a thicket and found himself in the open with a clear view of the Indians and the rider. The man had fallen and was surrounded by four mounted braves. The fifth stood over their victim and was taking aim with an arrow. All five were armed with bows.

Fargo whipped the Sharps to his shoulder but before he could squeeze the trigger he saw the fifth brave send the shaft into the downed man's abdomen. Scowling in anger, he released the reins and rode by the pressure of his thighs and legs alone, freeing his hands to shoot. Trying to sight while at a full gallop was difficult and only the best marksmen could do it, yet he barely hesitated as he took a bead and fired.

Two hundred yards distant the fifth Paiute threw up his hands and collapsed. Immediately the rest turned toward the source of the shot, vented whoops of fury, and urged their ponies to the attack.

Fargo fed another round into the chamber, sighted on the foremost Paiute, and fired again. The blast of the powerful gun rolled off across the plain and the Paiute pitched headfirst to the hard earth.

The remaining three swerved to the east, making for a stand of trees. Their bows were no match for the new-comer's deadly rifle and they well knew it. They were still a score of yards from safety when a third shot toppled a third brave, and once the surviving pair reached the trees they kept on going. Revenge on the whites was one thing, certain suicide quite another.

Skye slowed as he neared the hapless rider. There were two arrows protruding from the man's stomach. Such shafts, tipped as they were with barbed points that tore a man's insides as badly as a bullet, often caused a lingering, exquisitely painful death. And frequently Indians dipped their arrows in rattlesnake venom or the livers of dead animals so any puncture would spread poison into the system as well as rip and tear, making the shafts even more lethal.

He held no hope for the rider although the man's right arm was moving feebly. The horse had tripped in a shallow hollow and broken a leg. It lay on its side, breathing heavily, its eyes wide with fright.

The rider turned his head at the sound of the Ovaro's hoofs and looked up, his youthful features etched with acute agony. Relief temporarily replaced the torment when he realized it was a white man and not the Paiutes. He licked his thin lips, then croaked out, "Need . . . help."

Fargo glanced at the trees to make sure the war party had gone, then swung to the ground and crouched next to the young man. Closer inspection verified his earlier assessment. Both arrows were in deep and the man's buckskin shirt was soaked with blood. "There's not much I can do for you," he admitted softly.

The man nodded. "I know," he said, his voice weak. A trickle of blood formed at the corner of his mouth.

"Would you care for some water?" Fargo asked.

"No," the young man replied. "Need help."

Fargo thought the man must be in shock. He'd just told him there was nothing he could do. "There's no doctor for hundreds of miles," he said. "And if I try to take out those arrows you'll bleed faster and die sooner."

The rider gave a slight shake of his head and grimaced. "Not me. The mail."

"The what?" Fargo asked, wondering if he had heard correctly.

"The mail. Get it to the next station."

Fargo looked at the stricken horse again and blinked in surprise. He should have seen it sooner. The animal was fitted with a unique saddle few men had ever straddled, the distinctive, lightweight, stripped down kind used exclusively by an outfit that had only been in business slightly over a month. And draped over the saddle was a leather rectangle known as a *mochila* with a mail pouch called a *cantina* at each corner. "You ride for the Pony Express," he declared.

"Yes," the rider said.

Stories about the fledgling mail service were in all the newspapers and being discussed in every saloon and around every campfire in the West. Started by the freighting firm of Russell, Majors, and Waddell, the Pony Express was a bold enterprise being conducted on a grand scale. A chain of riders now carried the mail from St. Joseph, Missouri to San Francisco in less than half the time required before the Express, as it was frequently dubbed, went into operation.

"Will you take it, mister?"

The question gave Skye pause. He wasn't an Express employee and wasn't obligated in any respect to complete the rider's run. But as he gazed at the young man's earnest expression and saw the silent appeal in the man's eyes, he had a change a heart.

All that he had heard about the Express riders flashed through his mind. They were all close to twenty years of age and lightly built. They were all tough and resilient and expert horsemen. Above all, they were all committed to the oath of loyalty they were required to take, a pledge of honesty and proper conduct.

"Please," the rider said.

Skye glanced at the *mochila*.

"The mail must go through," the young man stated, repeating the company slogan in a tone that made his statement an entreaty. "Please, mister."

"All right," Fargo agreed, wondering what he had let himself in for. "I'll take the mail to the next station."

A smile of gratitude creased the young man's lips. "Thanks. The next stop is Roberts Creek."

"What's your name?" Fargo asked. The words were no sooner spoken than the rider gasped, stiffened, and went limp. He put a hand on the man's wrist and felt for a pulse. There was none.

Sighing, Fargo stood and replaced the spent rounds in his rifle and the Colt. Roberts Creek wasn't all that far, perhaps ten miles all told, so dropping off the mail wouldn't entail much of a delay. He twirled the revolver into his holster, slid the Sharps into its scabbard, and stepped to the Express horse.

The animal looked up at him and whinnied. A jagged piece of bone jutted from the torn flesh in its front leg, which was bent at an unnatural angle.

Fargo leaned down and stripped the *mochila* off. He knelt and stroked the animal's neck, putting the horse at ease. In a minute the animal placed its head on the ground and wearily closed its eyes. Only then did Fargo ease the Colt out, touch the tip of the barrel to the gelding's forehead, and shoot. The horse barely quivered and was still.

"You deserved better," Fargo said softly, and stood. In a land where a man's life frequently depended on his mount, he appreciated a good horse as much as anyone. And the animals used by the Express were the best money could buy.

He carried the *mochila* to the Ovaro, then folded it in half and draped it on his saddle behind the cantle. Taking a length of rope from his saddlebags that he normally used when picketing the stallion, he tied the *mochila* securely.

A shadow flitted across the ground nearby. Fargo

*13*

pushed his hat back and glanced skyward. Already circling far overhead was a solitary buzzard. Given time, more would join it. He debated whether to bury the Pony Express rider and decided against it. In the first place he didn't have anything to dig with, and in the second place the Paiutes might get the notion to swing around and try their luck again.

Reluctantly, he climbed onto the stallion and headed out, riding due west. In short order he crossed the wash and went a mile over a dry flat. The ground baked like an oven, reflecting waves of heat, and sweat trickled down his back.

As he rode he was constantly alert. Where there were five Paiutes there might well be more, and that smoke signal was bound to attract others. The Paiutes had never been regarded as an especially fierce tribe, but desperation had driven them to extreme measures.

Always among the poorest of tribes, the Paiutes subsisted on whatever the harsh land had to offer, which wasn't much. In the winter they lived on a meager diet of small game. In early spring they ate the first fresh plants, particularly cattails which the women gathered by the hundreds. Through the rest of the spring and summer they hunted ducks, caught fish, and collected wild rice. Come the fall and their diet changed to pine nuts and rabbit meat. They never had a surplus of food and often went hungry for days at a time.

Then along came the white man. As usual, the whites had little regard for the natives and treated them with disdain. As usual, the whites hunted and fished to their hearts' content, taking a large portion of what little food the land had to offer for themselves. The Paiutes found themselves in competition with the hordes of migrating whites and didn't like it one bit. To the whites it was a matter of filling their bellies on their way west. To the Paiutes it was a matter of tribal survival.

The last straw, or so Skye had heard, came when the whites took to hacking down piñon trees for wood, the very trees the Paiutes depended on for their nuts in the fall. On top of that, the previous winter had been bitterly cold with many fierce blizzards. The Paiutes suffered terribly, and they blamed all of their suffering on the white man.

So recently war had erupted, and so far the Paiutes were holding their own. They had raided a number of Express stations, remote ranches, and isolated communities, slaying dozens before the whites even realized the Paiutes were on the warpath.

Then came the disastrous battle of Pyramid Lake. A volunteer force of 105 men, recruited from Carson City, Virginia City, Genoa, and other towns, assembled and marched out to punish the Paiutes for their transgressions. Unfortunately, because they viewed the Indians with contempt, they marched boldly up to a Paiute encampment at Pyramid Lake and into as perfect a trap as was ever conceived by any Indians anywhere. Almost half of the whites were slain before the rest fled in stark panic. Later, the Paiutes would say that many of the white men cried like little papooses as the warriors swarmed among them and were as easy to run down and kill as cattle.

Fargo had been told in Salt Lake City that a new effort was soon to be mounted against the Paiutes. This one would be better organized and would be led by an experienced military officer. But until then, until the Paiute uprising was contained, any white man or woman venturing west of Salt Lake City did so with no guarantee they would ever arrive in California.

A drumming noise from the rear shattered Skye's reflection and he looked back over his shoulder to see the pair of Paiutes who had gotten away earlier along with twenty of their furious tribesmen rushing to overtake him.

## 2

Fargo calmly regarded the onrushing swarm of savages for a moment, then touched his spurs to the Ovaro. The stallion had been in similar situations with him many times before and it knew exactly what to do, which was to break into a full run in the blink of an eye. He bent low to decrease the wind resistance and aid the Ovaro in maintaining an even stride and balance.

The Paiutes burst into furious cries and waved their weapons overhead. All of them were eager to avenge the lives of their fellow braves. They viciously goaded their mounts on with their heavy quirts in an attempt to rapidly overtake the big white man in the buckskins and white hat.

Fargo was several hundred yards in front of the war party and slowly increasing the distance. He rode effortlessly, an extension of his superb horse. Unless the Ovaro tripped in a hole or rut as had the Pony Express rider's animal, he had little to worry about. Not only was the Ovaro one of the fastest horses he'd ever owned or seen, he had also taken a standard precaution that added immensely to the stallion's speed and stamina.

It was a trick the Pony Express used, the reason they could send out their young riders armed with just a single Colt. Their horses, like the Ovaro, were fleet of foot and justifiably so, but there was more to it than that. Because the operators of the Express knew the same secret Fargo had learned when still a boy, a secret every horseman worthy of the name practiced regularly, a secret so simple and yet so effective.

Long ago someone had discovered that grain-fed horses invariably performed better than those fed on grass. Even when all else was equal, a horse sustained on a steady grain diet could run faster than one fed on grass. So the Pony Express went to the extra expense of feeding their mounts grain.

Whenever Fargo could, he did the same. Out on the prairie or in the mountains he had to get by with grass, but when he stopped in a town and bedded the stallion at a livery he always directed that it be fed grain. In Salt Lake City, knowing what lay ahead, he had tarried for a few days so the Ovaro would get to have much more grain than usual. And now his foresight was paying off handsomely.

He skirted a cluster of mesquite, leaped a narrow gully, and spied a butte ahead. Many boulders were strewn along its base and they gave him an idea. Shucking the Sharps from its scabbard, he made for a gap between a pair of boulders each as big as a house. A glance back showed the Paiutes had not yet appeared around the mesquite.

In a swirl of dust Fargo rode into the gap and vaulted from the saddle. Spinning, he braced his shoulder against the left-hand boulder and raised the rifle.

Still whooping and waving their bows and lances, the Paiute band swept into the open. They were almost to the gully before they realized it was there and the leading warriors automatically slowed a bit as they gauged its width and prepared to jump it.

Fargo had counted on them to do just that, giving him a fraction of a second longer to take careful aim. His first shot nailed a tall brave at the center of the pack and the man fell into the gully as his war horse leaped. A second shot bored through a stocky Paiute who landed on the near side. Again he fired, and this time an elderly warrior on the fringe of the bunch clutched at his chest and became another casualty.

The remaining Paiutes were thrown into confusion by the unexpected tactic. Since the three shots had boomed so close together, many of them believed there must be more than one white man in the boulders. None of them knew that a skilled shooter could fire four or five shots a minute with a Sharps. In Fargo's case it was six rounds in sixty seconds, and four of them were dead before the rest bore to the right or left heading for the nearest cover.

Skye tracked a fifth warrior with his sight, led the man

a hair, and squeezed off a shot. The man's head snapped back, spraying crimson, and the ground claimed him.

Scattering, the rest of the war party went to ground.

So much for his delaying tactic, Fargo reflected, and ran to the Ovaro. Swinging up, he yanked on the reins and threaded a hasty path among the boulders until he reached the north side of the butte. A look sufficed to discover the Paiutes were still hidden, probably regrouping and debating their next move. Grinning, he dashed around the end of the butte and into the valley to the west. By the time they became aware of his ruse he would be miles away.

He held the Ovaro to a trot in case the Paiutes were smarter than he reckoned and took up the chase sooner than he expected. Then he might need all the speed the Ovaro could muster. The stallion was hardly fazed by its exertions so far and forged on tirelessly.

Fargo kept a watchful eye on the surrounding countryside. Should there be more Paiutes in the area he wanted to see them before they saw him.

The chase had detoured him to the north of the trail he must take to reach Roberts Creek by the shortest route so he swung in a loop and approached the station from the northeast. Although he had never been there before he had no difficulty finding it.

A column of dark smoke pinpointed the exact site.

Out came the Sharps. Fargo rested it across his legs and loosened the Colt in its holster. He knew what he would find but he fervently hoped he was wrong. Coming out on a rise he reined up and somberly scanned the canyon below.

Whoever picked the site had done a fine job. The newspapers had reported that as much care went into the selection of a station outpost as went into the selection of the horses for the Express riders, and it showed here. In this instance the station had been constructed near the creek and close to a flourishing tract of junipers, piñon pines, and willow trees. Their ready availability accounted for the fact this particular station had been built of wood and not adobe as was the case with most of the stations west of Salt Lake City.

Huge beams had been used to support the roof, and those beams now lay in a tangled, smoldering heap, giving off much of the black smoke spiraling upward on the sluggish currents. South of the station building was a corral. Part of the fence had been torn down, no doubt to allow the stock to be driven off.

Fargo cautiously went down a game trail to the bottom of the canyon. Staying in the trees, he moved slowly forward. The station had been hit not more than two hours ago, perhaps by the same war party that had tried to catch him. He tried to remember how many personnel the Express assigned to each station and seemed to recall the number varied depending on the size and location. He doubted there had been more than the station keeper and a couple of stock tenders present when the Paiutes struck.

It was conceivable the Express employees had escaped. If they had somehow seen the war party close in, they would have ridden off as fast as they could saddle their animals. But knowing Indians as he did, knowing how stealthy they could be when on a raid, he expected to find bodies close to the ruins.

He did. At the tree line he halted and saw a prone figure lying within yards of the building. Four arrows were imbedded in the man's back and his scalp had been taken. So, oddly, had his boots, possibly by a brave who intended to cut them up and use the leather for another purpose. A wild Indian would never wear a white man's boots, not for all the whiskey in the world. More than one warrior had remarked to Fargo that they couldn't comprehend why white men liked to clump around in heavy footwear when they could walk lightly and comfortably in moccasins.

Only when he was fully satisfied there were no Indians lurking in the vicinity did Fargo emerge from the woods. He made a complete circuit of the station and saw where the war party had ridden off to the east. Nowhere was there any indication Paiutes were nearby.

East of the corral, lying on his back in a gully, was a man who might have worked as a stock tender. His throat had been slit, his eyes gouged out, and his hair lifted.

Skye now doubted any of the Express employees had escaped. He found where several shod horses had been driven off by five Indians toward the south and guessed the station stock was being taken to the Paiute encampment. Between the loss of lives, the burned structure, and the stolen horses, the Pony Express had sustained a considerable loss. If the Paiutes kept this up all along the line, the Express faced huge financial losses.

He halted near the first body he'd seen, hooked a leg over the saddle horn, and pondered. In order to deliver the mail as he'd promised the dying rider, he must now head for the next station and hope it wasn't in the same condition. Racking his memory, he recalled that Dry Creek Station was the name of the next stop. If he rode hard he might arrive there by nightfall. Then he could hand over the *mochila* and go about his own business.

Having made up his mind, Fargo lowered his leg into the stirrup, slipped the Sharps into its scabbard, and lifted the reins to turn the stallion.

Abruptly, from near the smoldering building, there came a distinct thud.

Bright sunlight glinted off the Colt's barrel as Fargo palmed the gun and twisted, his thumb pulling back the hammer before the revolver was level. He detected a flicker of movement low to the ground on the west side of the ruins and a few swirls of dust rose into the air. If it was Paiutes, the smartest move would to be take the fight to the them and try to drive them back, then wheel and skedaddle.

He urged the Ovaro into a run, reached the southwest corner, and drew rein. Not so much as a lizard stirred on the flat stretch leading to Roberts Creek. Nor was there anyone in the trees. Mystified, he rode a few feet until the stallion's front hoof struck the ground with a dull thump. Instantly, he yanked on the reins, turning the horse aside.

The ground had been stripped of grass and weeds by the passage of horses and wagons, and a fine layer of dust covered the earth. As his eyes roved over that dirt, he noticed a flat piece of lumber had been partially exposed. He dismounted, keeping the Colt out, and squatted next to the board.

Using his left hand, Fargo brushed more dirt aside and exposed more boards in the process. In a minute he had uncovered an entire door lying flat in the soil and found an iron ring used to lift one side. He grasped the ring, bunched his shoulder muscles, and began to lift. The door rose an inch, and from underneath there issued an audible metallic click. Then another.

Fargo let go and threw himself backward, none too soon. Twin blasts sounded, muffled by the door, and large sections of the wood exploded upward. A flying sliver stung his left cheek and another nicked his neck. He lay with his elbows propped, watching gunsmoke waft from the jagged holes.

In the silence attending the gun blasts, a voice whispered under the door. "Do you reckon you nailed him?"

"I reckon," someone else answered in harsh satisfaction. "There's one less Paiute bastard in the world."

"But they know we're here."

"Maybe there was just one."

"Paiutes always travel in packs like wolves."

"Then we'll take some more with us before we die."

Fargo had heard enough. He rose to his knees and shook his head in amazement, then coughed and said, "You ladies can come out from down there if you want. I'm not a Paiute, but you came damn close to parting my hair with that shotgun of yours."

"Who said that?" one of the women blurted.

"It might be a dirty Paiute trick," said the other.

"Since when do Paiutes speak English?" demanded the first one.

"Some Sioux and Cheyenne and Blackfeet have learned English. Why couldn't a dumb Paiute?"

"I want to take a peek."

"Forget it. We're safe here."

"A peek won't hurt."

"No."

"Why are you always so bossy?"

"Because I'm the one with brains."

Rising, but staying well clear of the door, Fargo slid the Colt into his holster and brushed dust from his buckskins. "If you ladies want to spend the rest of your lives down there, suit yourselves. But I'm riding out shortly and there might not be another white man by this way for weeks."

His announcement brought more whispering.

"He says he's a white man."

"Paiutes can lie just like anyone else."

"But what if he's telling the truth?"

"Do you want to risk losing your hair? Or, worse, being forced to live with a grubby Injun the rest of your days, eating dog meat and raising a passel of breed brats?"

"Not all Injuns eat dog meat."

"How would you know? Have you ever lived with any?"

"There was that old Injun who worked at the livery. He came in every now and then and I took a shine to him. As polite a man you seldom did see. And neat! He always folded his drawers before—."

"Shhh. I think he's listening to us."

"Who?"

"The gent up there, you idiot."

Their voices became too low to hear. Fargo folded his arms and waited. As near as he could figure, below that door was a root cellar or just a plain hole the station keeper had dug to store food or whatever. Perhaps the man had seen the Paiutes coming and managed to conceal the women down there before the attack. Then the keeper or the stock tender had spread dirt over the door to hide it from the Indians. Maybe that delay had enabled the Paiutes to catch the two men flat-footed and in the open. Those women, whether they realized it or not, might owe their lives to the sacrifice of the Express employees.

"Mister?" one of the women called.

"I'm still here," Fargo responded.

"We're coming out. I don't trust you one bit, so I want you to stand still when we do. Move toward us and I'll put a hole in you large enough to ride a horse through. Savvy?"

"You're in no danger from me."

"We'd better not be. I may not be gun-handy with a six-shooter, but this shotgun Mr. Delaney gave me is real easy to aim."

"Come on out," Fargo prompted, and held perfectly still as someone applied leverage below and the door started to swing up on squeaky recessed hinges nailed into a narrow beam buried beside it. The twin shotgun barrels poked out and pointed in his direction.

"Not a move, mister."

"My hair will be gray by the time you show your-selves," Fargo retorted. He heard more whispering, then the door was shoved all the way open and out climbed the woman bearing the shotgun, her companion right behind her. They stood side by side and regarded him critically.

For his part, Fargo could have been floored with a feather duster. He hadn't known what to expect; perhaps a couple of women from a nearby ranch if there was one or the wife and daughter of the station keeper or the stock tender. Instead, standing before him were two lovely ladies in fine, low-cut dresses that amply revealed their ample cleavage. The woman holding the shotgun was a blonde, her friend a brunette.

"Look at those shoulders," the brunette cooed.

The blonde didn't take her eyes off Fargo when she replied, "This isn't the proper time or place, Lida. I swear you don't have the common sense God gave a turnip."

Lida opened her mouth to say something when her gaze strayed to the body of the man near the station and instead of words out came a horrified squeal.

Startled, the blonde glanced in the direction her friend was looking and inadvertently lowered the shotgun a few inches.

Which gave Skye the opening he needed. He didn't like having those twin barrels pointed at his middle. The woman's finger rested lightly on one of the triggers, and all it would take was a nervous twitch of her hand and he'd be blown in half. So the moment she was distracted he took a quick step, his right hand closing on the shot-gun and twisting it sharply upward. Her finger started to tighten, but with a wrench he tore the weapon from her grasp and took a step back.

"Damn you!" the blonde hissed, clenching her slender hands into small fists.

Lida still gaped at the corpse.

"Sorry, ma'am," Fargo said. "But I aim to live a few more years, at least." He hefted the shotgun, a fine percussion 12-gauge made in England and sporting a walnut stock with a checkered grip. The gun was five to ten years old but had been well cared for. "If I give this back to you, I want your word that you won't point it at me again."

"How do I know I can trust you?"

Fargo gave her his friendliest carefree smile. "I reckon you'll have to take me on good faith."

"Mister, I learned long ago that the woman who puts her faith in a man she's just met is asking for grief. Men are like horses, my ma always said. A gal should study their gait before she gets in the saddle."

Fargo couldn't help but laugh. "What's your name?"

"Rosemary Griffin. This here is Lida Strippgen."

"If you don't mind my asking, what are two such ladies as yourselves doing way out here in the middle of nowhere?"

Rosemary had been examining his face as if she'd never seen one before. She relaxed at last, letting her fingers uncurl, and answered, "Lida and I were on our way from Denver to San Francisco. We got as far as this station and then Mr. Delaney told the stage driver the Paiutes had been prowling about in this area. Delaney and Meeker were fixing to light out for Salt Lake City when our stage showed up."

Skye stared at the smoke rising from the beams. Since the stage route closely paralleled the route taken by the Express riders, stages stopped regularly at Express stations. The Express management didn't mind since the company made a little extra money selling food to hungry passengers and the isolated station keepers were always glad for some company.

"Delaney was the station keeper?" Fargo guessed.

"Yep." Rosemary nodded at the body. "That's him over there." She frowned, her features softening. "He was a nice man. Went out of his way to make us comfortable."

There were a few questions Fargo wanted to ask her to clarify what had happened, but before he could Lida jerked her arm up and pointed to the east.

"Is that a dust devil?"

Fargo turned, his right hand dropping to his Colt. The billowing cloud of fine dust not a mile off wasn't the result of freak winds. "No," he told them. "The Paiutes are coming back."

# 3

"They'll kill us!" Lida wailed.

"Not if I can help it," Fargo assured her. His questions would have to wait until a better time. "Come with me," he directed, and stepped to the Ovaro. Gripping the bridle, he led the stallion into the creek, then turned northward and walked for a hundred yards before slanting into a cluster of willows on the creek bank.

The women had dutifully followed, neither saying a word. Of the two, Rosemary was the more composed. Lida's pale face testified to her terror and she repeatedly wrung her hands in her dress.

Once in the trees, Fargo turned due north. Except for the occasional chirping of birds, the woods were silent. It would be a couple of minutes yet before the Paiutes arrived at the station. They would either ride right up or they might hang back and observe it for a while before moving in. He hoped they did the former. If they were in a hurry to catch him, they might not notice his fresh tracks and those of the women. They might assume he had gone on toward the next station and they would do the same.

Eventually the trees thinned out and before him wound the game trail to the top of the canyon. "We're going up," he announced. "It's not very steep and you shouldn't have any difficulty."

"But I'm so tired," Lida complained. "We were in that hole for hours without any food or water. I need a rest."

"Be my guest," Fargo said. "But Rosemary and I aren't stopping. And if those Paiutes find our tracks they'll be here in no time." He paused to give her a chance to dwell on that, then added, "Do you have any idea what they do to white women?"

Lida glanced at her companion, who stared straight

ahead, and her slim shoulders slumped. "All right. Lead the way."

"Here," Fargo said, and handed the shotgun to Rosemary. "If the war party finds us, I'll probably have my hands full. Was I you, I'd save those shells for Lida and you."

"You mean kill ourselves?" Lida said in astonishment.

"Either that or let the Paiutes do it for you, only they'll likely rape you first and then torture you to see if you have courage or not."

Rosemary looked thoughtfully at the gun, then at Skye. "I'll do whatever is necessary."

Nodding, Fargo led the stallion along the trail. Once they were on top he would let the women ride and he would have to walk. Not that a long trek across the bleak terrain appealed to him. He would rather they all had mounts, but the only other horses for miles around belonged to the Paiutes. The thought gave him an idea.

When they were above the treetops he looked toward the station and saw the thinning column of smoke. The war party must be there by now. Fortunately, the trees screened them from the Paiutes' view.

Working his way ever higher, Skye repeatedly scanned the land below. If the Indians rode westward they would soon be visible, but so far they had not appeared. Which was not good. The Paiutes undoubtedly were scouring the ground for his tracks and would soon take up the chase once more.

Below the rim he paused to verify no Indians were watching, and then he took the Ovaro up and over. The women climbed nimbly and stood on the edge breathing heavily from their exertion.

"Don't skyline yourselves like that," Fargo advised, taking the Ovaro a dozen steps before stopping. "The Paiutes will have an excellent target."

Both women reacted as if they were standing on tacks and moved to his side.

"Now what?" Rosemary inquired. "With only one horse we don't stand a chance of eluding them."

"Maybe we can get a couple more," Fargo said, shucking the Sharps from the boot. He pointed at the mouth to a draw thirty yards to the northwest. "Take my stallion there and wait. When I wave, come on the run."

"What are you going to do?" Lida asked.

"Reduce the odds some," Fargo answered, and walked to the rim where he squatted and aligned the rifle across his thighs. Not five seconds later he detected movement below. A line of Paiutes was riding toward the canyon wall, their eyes on the ground as they followed the Ovaro's fresh tracks and those of the women. Fargo had left few prints himself. Long ago he had learned to move like an Apache, to tread so lightly his feet barely smudged the soil.

He went prone, removed his hat, and raised his head until his eyes cleared the rim. From the canyon floor it would be impossible to distinguish him from the many small boulders and large rocks to his right and left.

The lead Paiute halted and the rest did the same. Several joined the first warrior and an animated discussion ensued. Now and again one of them would jab a finger at the top of the canyon.

They were debating whether to take the trail up or swing around, Fargo deduced. On the narrow trail they would be vulnerable, exposed to gunfire from above. None of them would care to ride into an ambush.

On the other hand, the warriors might decide that their quarry was fleeing in unreasoning fear and would likely be a mile away by this time. If the war party went around, they would lose valuable time. Going up the trail to the rim was the quickest way.

Fargo smiled when he saw the apparent leader gesture at the trail and begin the ascent. Using his elbows and knees he scrambled back until it was safe to stand, then donned his hat and took refuge behind a waist-high boulder on his left. Kneeling, he bent at the waist and rested his forehead on the dry earth, molding his body to the shape of the boulder. The Paiutes would have no idea he was there until it was too late unless one of their horses got his scent and alerted its rider.

Sweat trickled down his back and dust got into his nostrils. The waiting seemed to last forever. He was beginning to wonder if the Paiutes had changed their minds when he heard a horse snort from somewhere just below the rim.

He thought of the women, and on an impulse inched his face along the bottom of the boulder until he could see the draw. Flabbergasted, he saw Rosemary and Lida standing at its mouth, in the open, Rosemary holding the Ovaro. Of all the harebrained dunderheads he'd ever met, those two were at the top of the list! They hadn't even bothered to conceal themselves!

Fargo almost uncoiled and waved for them to take cover, but the clump of a hoof as a horse cleared the canyon top alerted him to the arrival of the lead Paiute. He heard a surprised exclamation, and then the horse broke into a gallop. The leader had spied the women.

Another horse came over the lip and the Paiute called something down to those behind him, then urged his mount into a run.

Two horses were all they needed. Fargo straightened to find the leader already twenty yards away and the second Paiute half that distance. A third warrior was just appearing. He snapped the Sharps up and banged off a shot, his slug ripping through the third warrior's forehead.

The warrior's brains and hair exploded out the back of his head and arced toward the canyon floor. A moment later the warrior toppled and imitated their example.

Sprinting, Fargo reached the edge and drew his Colt. The riderless horse had stopped in a panic and the Paiutes behind it were angrily trying to get it moving since there wasn't enough space for them to go around. A number of them looked up in consternation when Fargo suddenly materialized.

He fired three times, snapping shots at the next three braves in line. Each shot sent a warrior hurtling toward the boulders far below. Several others brought their bows or rifles to bear, but the angle was too steep for them to aim accurately and their horses wouldn't stand still. An arrow streaked past his shoulder and a bullet smacked into a rock beside him.

The four riderless animals were trying to flee. Lacking room to turn, they were backing down the trail and throwing the war ponies behind them into confusion. The Paiutes bellowed and cursed. One man was unable to control his slipping horse and both pitched over the edge, the man screaming until he crashed into a stone slab at the base of the canyon wall.

Fargo spun, bringing the Colt up. The leader and the second warrior were charging, each pulling the string back on his bow. He dropped the nearest threat as the second warrior let his shaft fly and the arrow nicked his hat in passing.

Shrieking his fury, the leader let go of the nock and his shaft sped straight at Fargo's chest. Skye twisted sharply. Whizzing like an angry hornet, the arrow missed him by a hair, the buzzard feather brushing his shirt. Not bothering to take conscious aim, he instinctively pointed the .44 at the onrushing warrior and emptied his revolver.

Two holes blossomed at heart level and the brave slumped, then tumbled, his bow flying from his lifeless fingers.

Fargo moved to the rim again. Below was a scene of total pandemonium, with horses whinnying and warriors shouting. Somehow, one of the riderless mounts near the top had managed to turn and was trying to force its way down. The Paiutes below couldn't get past. Those braves closest to the bottom, where the trail broadened, had retraced their steps and were watching the bedlam above them in grim apprehension. Another horse and rider had fallen and were lying on the slope, the warrior pinned by his mount.

He gave the signal for the women to hurry back. Neither of the Indian ponies on top had gone more than a dozen yards, so if he could catch them quickly and leave he stood to gain a substantial lead on the Paiutes.

Skye tucked the Sharps under one arm and hastily reloaded the Colt, all the while marking the efforts of the war party to gain the rim. So far the Indians were failing. Eventually, though, the persistent braves would accomplish their objective. He must be out of rifle and bow range by then.

The women reached him as he slid a fifth bullet into his Colt. He shoved the gun at Rosemary and said, "Don't let any of them get over the rim."

"But I've never killed a man before."

"Haven't you heard? There's always a first time for everything," Fargo told her, turning. Afraid the Indian mounts would spook and run off, he approached the nearest one slowly. "There, there, boy. Don't go anywhere."

Up went the animal's tapered ears but it made no attempt to shy away.

"I won't hurt you," Fargo assured it, counting on his calm voice to soothe the horse enough for him to grab the rope bridle. Even if the language was unfamiliar, the tone would not be. He held his right arm loosely, his fingers slightly curled.

The war horse bobbed its head, its nostrils flaring, but it made no move to flee.

"See? I told you," Fargo said, smiling, and was finally near enough to reach up and take the reins. He made no quick movements for fear of sparking flight. "Can you ride?" he asked over his shoulder.

"I could ride when I was four," Rosemary bragged. "And I've ridden bareback many a time."

"I'm not much good on horses," Lida said timidly. "They've always scared me to death."

"You don't have any choice," Fargo stated. "If we double up the Paiutes will overtake us eventually. Climb on this one. I'll give you a boost."

Lida wrung her hands and offered a tentative smile to the watchful bay. "Nice horsey," she said as would a nervous little girl. "Be a nice horsey and don't throw me. Please."

"Here," Fargo said, leaning the Sharps against his leg and lowering his right hand so she could step onto his palm. "Nice and easy does it."

"Oh, my," Lida said. She glanced at the dead Paiutes, then took a breath, placed her dainty foot in his hand, and allowed herself to be perched on the bay. Her hands trembled slightly as she gripped the reins.

"You'll be all right," Fargo encouraged her. He was glad both women had on dresses that were loose and flowing from the waist down. Otherwise they would have to ride sideways, which was a damned uncomfortable way to ride across the rugged country they would shortly be crossing. Scooping up the Sharps, he turned to go get the second Indian mount. To his surprise, Rosemary was walking toward it and speaking just as he had.

The big horse let her approach, its eyes on her golden

hair. It didn't try to move off when she placed a hand on its neck and rubbed gently.

"She's always had a way with animals," Lida said.

Fargo waited for Rosemary to climb up, then he hastened to the Ovaro, slid the Sharps into the scabbard, and stepped into the stirrups. He moved to the canyon rim. Most of the Paiutes were now at the bottom, the rest were on their way. A tall brave spied him and shouted a warning.

One of the warriors on the trail shifted to bring a rifle into play.

Skye shot him off his horse. Then, wheeling the pinto, he rode to the northwest. Both women fell in beside him, Rosemary riding easily, Lida as tense as could be.

He reasoned that the war party would spend time debating their course of action. None of them would want to risk the trail to the rim again, and they would probably seek another place where they could gain the top without being picked off like sitting ducks. All of which would give him and the two women time to make their getaway.

Somehow, he must lose the war party. There were bound to be excellent trackers among the band, and shaking them would be an extremely difficult task. Born and bred in a wild land where their very survival often depended on their ability to read sign, most Indians could read tracks as well as the average white man could read a book. And some were outstanding, able to tell from a crease in the soil or the bend of a patch of grass exactly what had left the spoor.

Fargo was no greenhorn at tracking, either. He'd spent so much time among Indians that he could read prints as well as they could, even better than most. And his skill at trailing man or beast, as well as other, deadlier skills he possessed, had earned him quite a reputation.

In a day and age when the latest news and gossip was bandied about at every saloon and tavern west of the Mississippi, it was natural for Western men to talk of those matters that interested them the most; the latest Indian raids, cattle and gold prices, quality horseflesh, and fights of any sort but particularly gunfights. Such men lived hard, uncompromising lives, and they never knew when they might be called upon to face a hostile Indian or a money-hungry hard case. So they wanted to hear stories about those who had been in similar situations, to listen and to learn and, to a great extent, to be entertained, for the stories told at the bars and around the gambling tables were the main entertainment these men had. Theaters were few and far between, and other than a good book or interesting conversation there was little a man could do to amuse himself.

As Fargo was aware, many of the stories circulating among the townsmen, ranchers, miners, and other hardy pioneers were about him. Not that he sought such notoriety. But in his wide travels he had run into more than his share of Indians and ruthless men who preyed on the innocent and the weak, men who had tried to prey on him and wound up as buzzard bait for their efforts. Inevitably, the tales of his wanderings had become as widespread as his travels themselves. It was little wonder he was often referred to as the Trailsman.

He thought of all this now because he would need all of his skill to get the two women to safety. His wisest course of action was to reach the next station. If it hadn't been burned and the Express employees slain, there would be hot food and shelter. There might even be someone who could escort the women westward to safety in California, because he had no desire to go so far with them. He liked to ride alone.

Plus there was the little matter of the *mochila* he still carried. Legally, it wasn't his responsibility and he was under no obligation to see that the mail went through other than his word to a dying man. But that was enough. Back East a man might be a chronic liar and cheat and still be able to mingle in polite society. Out here a man was measured by his reliability, and a man who always broke his word wound up shunned or despised. He'd promised to deliver the *mochila* and he would.

He stuck to level ground so the horses could run faster, disliking the dust they raised while hoping the Paiutes were still in the canyon and couldn't see it. Four miles or better fell behind them. Then four more. He spotted a narrow, rocky canyon where the ground was solid stone and their horses wouldn't leave any tracks at all. Motioning for the women to follow him, he rode several hundred yards into the canyon until he came to where it forked.

He took the left branch. The Paiutes, when they came, would be forced to check each fork separately or divide up. Either way, he would gain more ground and time.

The canyon widened out into a high, arid plain, and Fargo drew rein to give the horses a breather. The women had been too busy riding to speak a word, and they sat their horses wearily, unaccustomed to the heat and the long spell on horseback. All around them were jumbled rocks and boulders.

"I need something to drink," Lida panted.

Fargo reached for his canteen when from under a flat rock near her horse came a sound that chilled his blood, the loud buzzing of a rattlesnake's tail.

# 4

The horse bolted.

Indian mounts were accustomed to a wild, dangerous life. They were ridden over the roughest terrain imaginable, sometimes along trails where a single misstep would cause them to plummet hundreds or thousands of feet down a sheer cliff. Often they would have to go days without ample water or grass. At night they must be on their guard against mountain lions, grizzlies, and wolves. Not that Indian men didn't take excellent care of their animals. But by virtue of living in a vast wilderness where survival of the fittest was the order of things, an Indian mount developed outstanding reflexes or it didn't live to see old age. The horse Lida straddled was typical of the breed. At the first shake of the rattler's tail it took off, breaking into a gallop with its head held low and its tail flying. Lida squealed in terror and clung to its mane for dear life.

"Dammit," Fargo fumed, and spurred the Ovaro in pursuit. "Come on," he yelled to Rosemary, then melded his body to the pinto. The war horse was ten yards ahead and going flat out.

Lida was barely staying on. She swayed and bounced, her legs flapping, her head jerking, her hair tossed by the wind. "Help me!" she screamed. "Please help me!"

Scowling, Fargo poked his spurs into the Ovaro's ribs and listened to the clatter of the stallion's heavy hoofs. The ground was hard-packed and dotted with boulders and rocks. If Lida fell off at that speed she might sustain broken bones, or worse. He would be hard-pressed to nurse her and evade the roving bands of Paiutes at the same time.

"Hang on!" Rosemary cried.

He wished they would stop shouting. The war party,

or a different band, might be close by and hear. He looked to the north and south but saw no one, nor any dust.

Gradually the Ovaro gained. The stallion loved to let itself go now and again, to feel the vitality in its limbs and the air rushing past its face. It saw the chase as a challenge and rose to the occasion.

A minute later Skye was a mere two yards behind the Indian pony. Lida had slipped to one side and was on her stomach, her arms clamped around the animal's neck. She was in no position to haul on the reins even if he told her to do it. Exercising caution, he angled the Ovaro nearer and nearer until he was riding neck and neck with the war horse. Lunging, he grasped the bridle and yanked with all his strength.

The Paiute mount responded obediently and slowed. Side by side the two animals came to a stop.

Lida jumped off and sank to her knees. Shaking in abject fright, she clutched her thin arms to her chest, closed her eyes, and cried uncontrollably.

In a swirl of dust Rosemary arrived and leaped to the ground. She bent over her friend and draped an arm over Lida's quaking shoulders. "It's all right. You're safe now."

"I could have been killed!" Lida sputtered.

"But you weren't. So get ahold on yourself. We must keep going."

Lida looked up, her eyes brimming with tears and anger. "This is all your fault, Rose! Let's go to San Francisco, you said! The men are freer with their money and they know how to treat women like us. No more dirty miners or range riders who smell of horse sweat and cows." She sniffled. "You didn't say anything about Indians on the warpath. You didn't mention the fact we might be killed!"

"I never claimed the going would be easy. And, if you'll recall, we read in the papers about the Paiute uprising. We knew there might be a spot of trouble."

"A spot?" Lida declared, her voice wavering. "A spot! We're caught up in the middle of a war."

Fargo shifted, surveying the horizon, and spied a dust cloud to the southeast. "Ladies," he said softly, but neither of them paid him any mind.

"I don't want to go on to San Francisco," Lida snapped at Rosemary. "I want to go back. Denver wasn't all that bad, now that I think of it. Oh, some of the men didn't bathe regularly and they didn't always buy the best champagne or most expensive meals, but I wasn't mistreated. Madame Bovary wouldn't stand for that."

"Ladies," Fargo said again.

Rosemary put her hands on her hips and glared at Lida. "Since when did you take to liking Madame Bovary? She treated us like slaves, remember? We were never allowed to choose our men and always had to give her more than a fair percentage of the take. And for what? A two-bit room in a two-bit house where the sheets were only changed once a week and we were even charged for the cleaning bill."

"It wasn't that bad," Lida insisted, although her tone belied her statement.

Irritated, Fargo leaned down and bellowed. "Ladies! Get on your damn horses!"

They spun in unison.

"There's no need to be rude," Rosemary responded testily.

"After what I've just been through, you could at least be courteous," Lida added.

Skye jabbed a finger at the dust cloud. "And how courteous do you think the Paiutes will be?"

One look was enough to get them on their mounts. Fargo took the lead, simmering with annoyance. As if he didn't have enough to worry about, he would have to nursemaid the women every step of the way. Without him they wouldn't last a day, and with them the odds that he would get through to California were drastically reduced.

He made for a low mountain range to the southwest. If they followed it due south, they should find themselves close to Dry Creek Station. He saw a lizard streak under a flat rock to his right and in the sky a lone hawk soared.

Rosemary rode up beside him. "I'm sorry for all the trouble we're causing you."

"You're no trouble," Fargo growled.

She grinned. "In all the excitement I don't believe I caught your name."

"Fargo. Skye Fargo."

"I'm delighted to make your acquaintance. If you hadn't come along when you did I don't know what we would have done. We couldn't stay down in that hole much longer."

"You said the station keeper put you down there?"

"Yes. You see, the stage had stopped there and Mr. Delaney told the stage driver that an eastbound Express rider had reported seeing a large war party to the west, between Roberts Creek and Dry Creek Station. Delaney was worried the stage would ride right into them."

Fargo hadn't seen any sign of the stage and he could guess what had happened. "But the driver was all for going on anyway?"

Rosemary nodded. "Said he had to keep on, that it was his job. But Mr. Delaney persuaded Lida and I to wait for the next eastbound stage so we could go back to Salt Lake City until things cooled down." She sighed. "The stage hadn't been gone two minutes when we heard shooting to the west. Mr. Delaney figured the Paiutes had hit the stage and would hit the station next. So he gave me this shotgun and hustled us into that hole. Told us to stay put no matter what we heard."

"What did you hear?"

"For a long time, nothing. And then there was gunfire and the whoops of those savages. We could smell burning wood. After a while things quieted down. We were scared to death so we stayed huddled in the dark. Every so often one of us would lift the door to let in a little fresh air. And then you came along."

Fargo found himself noticing the way her large breasts rose and fell as she rode, pushing against the fabric and threatening to spill free at any second. The tight upper half of her dress left nothing at all to the imagination.

Rosemary saw where his eyes had drifted and her eyes twinkled as she said, "Like what you see, big man?"

"A man would have to be a fool not to."

Lida rode up from behind, staying close to her friend. "What are the two of you talking about?" she asked suspiciously.

"Mountains," Fargo replied, and saw Rosemary stifle laughter.

"I wish I was back in Denver," Lida said. "The mountains west of there are beautiful, covered with trees, and crisscrossed with pretty valleys." She made a sweeping gesture at the range toward which they were heading. "These, on the other hand, are bleak and ugly. How can anyone live in this godforsaken region?"

"What is beautiful to one person might be ugly to another," Fargo commented, twisting to check the location of the dust cloud. It seemed to be moving northwest. If the Paiutes were making it, they had spotted the dust being raised by the women and him. The Indians were on an intercept course to cut them off before they could reach Dry Creek Station.

"I know there are a few people ranching in this territory, but I'd never live out here," Lida said distastefully. "Have you seen what ranch life does to women? They look old before their time."

"Some do," Fargo conceded. "But so do some of the men. You've got to remember that ranchers and their wives live hard lives. They work from dawn to dusk seven days a week at backbreaking labor just to stay afloat. And they never know when a drought, disease, or a horde of locusts will come along and wipe them out. It takes tough people to make a go of it."

"You sound as if you admire them," Rosemary said.

"I admire anyone tough enough to carve out the kind of life they want to live no matter what the obstacles might be. Too many people never go after whatever it is they want most. They drift along with no real purpose. Anyone with grit, Indian or what, deserves respect. There are too many weaklings and vultures in this world as it is."

"My, my," Rosemary said. "A frontier philosopher."

"No," Fargo corrected her. "I've just been around and seen a lot."

"I'll bet you have."

He disregarded her sarcastic remark and studied the dust cloud again. The Paiutes were somewhere between a mile and two miles off. It was doubtful they would push their horses too hard in the blistering heat so for the moment he could devote his energies to eluding them rather than trying to outdistance them. But how? How in the world could he shake off some of the best trackers in existence?

A projecting arm of the range drew his attention.

There was bitter brush and mesquite there, as well as rabbit brush and a few stunted pines. A pale track led up and over the rise, a game trail of some sort.

"Stay close," Fargo said, and rode to the bottom of the slope. Impressed in the bare soil of the trail were the tracks of bighorn sheep, leading upward. He goaded the stallion to the top and halted to survey the land below.

The trail wound deeper into the range and disappeared around a distant bend. To the southeast the dust cloud wasn't any closer.

"Is this the way to the next station?" Lida asked skeptically.

"We'll get there eventually," Fargo answered.

"Eventually? The sooner we get there, the safer we'll be. Why aren't you taking us directly there?"

"Because that's what the Paiutes would expect. They know about the stages and the Express riders and they'll have bands watching the main trail. This way we might make it still owning our hair."

"I don't know if I like this."

"Quit your bitching," Rosemary said, and smiled at Fargo. "You do what you think is best. I trust you."

He stayed with the trail. Bighorn sheep were like mule deer; they drank water daily and seldom strayed all that far from their favorite watering hole. The trail might lead them to a spring or a tank.

Soon the Ovaro sniffed the air and increased its pace. So did the Indian ponies. He let the stallion have its head, and in less than five minutes they passed through a narrow gap between towering cliffs and emerged in a small meadow. A sparkling spring lay at the base of a talus slope.

"Oh, look!" Lida exclaimed, hurrying forward. Elated, she swung to the ground and knelt. Her hands were poised to dip into the cool liquid when a sharp command rang out.

"No. Let the horses drink first."

Lida glanced up in disbelief. "But my throat is parched! Why should I let my horse drink before me?"

"Our lives depend on our animals. We've been riding them hard for miles and they deserve first crack at that water," Fargo explained. Climbing down, he suited his words to action and let the Ovaro dip its muzzle into the spring.

"Damn it all," Lida muttered.

"You know he's right," Rosemary said. "So do it."

"Why the hell are you always taking his side, anyway?"

"Because I want to live."

All three mounts drank greedily, occasionally lifting their dripping muzzles to blow and toss their heads.

"Hurry it up, will you?" Lida groused.

Fargo said nothing. He had met her kind before, basically decent people who preferred the comforts of city life over all else. Comfort, in fact, was everything. They needed soft beds in which to sleep and delighted in hot meals at restaurants and the gaiety of the latest play or social function. They were city-born and city-bred, and once away from a city they were as much out of their element as a fish out of water.

At length Skye took the horses to one side so they could graze on the sparse grass near the spring. Both Rosemary and Lida were prone and gulping noisily when he returned. "Don't overdo it," he cautioned. "You'll give yourself a bellyache if you do."

"I don't care," Lida said, water spilling over her chin.

"You'll care if you can't ride and the Paiutes get their hands on you."

Lida glared at him and pushed herself to her knees. "Has anyone ever told you that you are a very depressing person? Don't do this! Don't do that! Just once I'd like to do something that meets with your approval."

"He'd have to wait ten years," Rosemary joked.

"Sit down and rest," Fargo advised. "You have five minutes until we mount up." He squatted, dipped his right hand in the spring, and slowly lifted a handful to his dry lips. The soothing water trickled down his throat, washing away the dust and discomfort.

Lida had walked off to sit in the shade of a boulder. Rosemary, though, had not moved an inch.

"I want you to know that one of us appreciates all you're doing."

"Thanks."

"Deep down Lida does, too. Only she's too stubborn to admit it. If it's any consolation, she's never satisfied.

Not even when everything is going her way. She always finds something to complain about."

"Why stick with her then?"

Rosemary shrugged. "We're best friends. Have been for almost ten years. Would you desert someone who was like a sister to you, the only family you ever had?"

Skye opened his mouth to answer when he saw the Ovaro lift its head and gaze back along the trail, its ear pricked. He quickly began filling his canteen and nodded at the war horses. "Mount up. Now."

"But you said we could have five minutes to rest?" Lida protested.

"We're about to have company. If you want to stay and greet them, be my guest."

Both women climbed on their animals without further argument.

As soon as the bubbles stopped gurgling from the canteen mouth, he stuck the cork in the neck and swiftly looped the strap over his saddle horn. Forking the pinto, he rode to the opposite end of the meadow and found a ridge leading down to a mesquite- and sage-covered canyon.

"Which way is Dry Creek Station?" Lida asked.

"Almost due south," Fargo said, moving along the ridge but staying below the crest. "Once we're out of this canyon we'll head straight for it."

"At last," Lida said.

Again and again Skye looked over his shoulder but saw no one emerge from the meadow. Once in the canyon the mesquite provided adequate concealment and they came to a plain without mishap.

"There's not much cover ahead," Rosemary remarked.

"If my hunch is right, we're not more than a mile from the station," Fargo informed them. "So we ride like hell until we get there. If the war party shows up I'll drop back and try to discourage them with my rifle. You two keep going no matter what."

"We won't abandon you," Rosemary said, her eyes locking on his.

"I can't hold them off and protect you at the same time," Fargo stated. He scoured the country one final time, then leaned over and gave her horse a slap on the rump. "Now ride, ladies, ride!"

# 5

For tense minutes they raced across the hot, dusty plain. Fargo had his Sharps out and ready but the Paiutes didn't appear. Puzzled, he tried putting himself in their moccasins to foresee their next move. He was certain the war party was close by and it troubled him that the Indians were holding back instead of attacking.

Dry Creek Station was aptly named. Constructed of adobe bricks, it had been situated on the west side of a dry creek in the shade of a few thin trees.

Fargo's pulse quickened when he saw the building and corral still intact. His elation was short-lived, however, when he realized there was no stock to be seen and the front door hung wide open. He let the women pound up to the station first, and he saw Lida suddenly jerk on the reins of her horse in alarm.

A body lay sprawled between the building and the corral, a lean man flat on his back with a halo of dried blood rimming his head and the front of his shirt stained bright red.

"Oh, no!" Lida wailed.

Fargo rode to the front door and slid from the saddle. The Paiutes had hit the station but they hadn't burned it to the ground as they had the one at Roberts Creek. Why not? Were they still here? Perhaps hidden inside to spring an ambush? "Wait here," he told the women, and advanced warily, the big rifle leveled.

The interior was in a shambles. Tables and chairs were upturned. Dishes had been shattered, pots and pans scattered. Every drawer had been emptied, the contents flung about. The Paiutes had taken everything they considered of value and left the rest.

"Skye!"

At Rosemary's cry Fargo raced out to discover her at the side of the station, her hand over her mouth. He ran to the corner and almost tripped over a second Express employee who was propped against the wall.

"He's alive," Rosemary said.

Fargo knelt. The man was young, not more than nineteen or twenty, and he had been shot to doll rags by arrows and bullets. Two shafts jutted from his stomach and there were three gaping holes in his chest. His eyes were closed, his chin touching his chest. "Mister?"

Incredibly, the man's eyes flicked open and took a bit to focus on Fargo. His lips moved feebly, croaking words. "Get out. Paiutes."

"I know," Fargo said.

"Name is Applegate. Tell my—"

And right then the man died, his breath escaping in a great sigh as his body slumped forward.

"Poor man," Rosemary said.

Fargo stood and gazed westward, trying to remember the name of the next station. Simpson's Park, he believed it was, but had it been attacked, too? The Paiutes seemed to be working their way east along the line, destroying one station after another.

"What do we do?" Lida inquired anxiously.

A good question, Fargo reflected. He squinted up at the sun, gauging there were less than two hours of daylight remaining. Their horses needed rest; so did they. And he didn't like the idea of trying to reach Simpson's Park in the dark. He wanted to be able to see the Paiutes when they closed in. "We'll spend the night here," he said.

"Is that wise?" Rosemary asked.

"The Paiutes have already been here once, and it's doubtful they'll come again unless the war party on our trail follows us here. They must be back at that spring and they probably won't come after us until daylight."

"But what if they do?" Lida wondered.

"The station walls are thick and there are plenty of loopholes to cover all the approaches. We'll be better off here than we would be anywhere else, and come morning we'll cut out for the next station."

"At least we can get a good night's sleep," Rosemary said.

Lida uttered an unladylike snort. "Who the hell can sleep at a time like this?"

"Why don't you two go in and tidy up?" Fargo proposed. "I'll bury the bodies and see to our horses."

"Shouldn't one of us keep watch while you're working?" Rosemary asked.

"I'll be fine, and I'd rather have you safe inside in case the Paiutes spring a surprise attack," Fargo said. He took their bridles, waited until they had dismounted and gone in, and led all three horses over to the small water tank beside the corral.

The locations of the Express stations had been established based on the distance a horse could go at top speed before flagging, and many had been constructed at arid sites lacking a stream or spring. At some stations wells had been dug at great expense to the firm. And where wells were impractical, water was hauled in using wagons. The barrels were then poured into a holding tank to reduce the evaporation rate and keep the water relatively fresh and cool.

He opened the tap at the bottom of the tank and water poured out into the trough. It was doubtful the Paiutes even knew what the tank contained unless they had spied on the employees and seen one water the stock. He let the water rise to the brim, then stopped the flow and permitted the horses to drink.

While the animals quenched their thirst, he stripped off his saddle, the *mochila*, and his gear. These he carried inside and deposited next to the door so they would be handy for a quick getaway. The women were busy sweeping debris into a corner and setting the furniture upright. Rosemary gave him a warm smile.

The bin of oats had not been touched, so he gave all three horses as much feed as he figured they could handle. They deserved it. He took a handful of hay and rubbed down the Ovaro but didn't bother doing the Indian ponies.

All the while he kept the Sharps nearby. Although he scoured in all directions again and again, he saw no dust clouds. As he was about to finish up with the Ovaro, he happened to glance at the station and was stunned to see gray smoke curling up from the chimney.

In a flash he snatched the rifle and raced inside. Lida

was on her knees in front of the potbelly stove, feeding short sections of a broken chair into slowly rising flames. "No!" he barked, and ran over. She took one look at his face and recoiled in fear. Ignoring her, he swiftly shoved the pieces aside with the barrel of the Sharps and the flames dwindled. So did the smoke.

"What's wrong?" Lida demanded. "I was only fixing to make supper."

"The smoke," Fargo said, stepping back and mopping his brow. "It can be seen for miles."

Lida stared at the stove, her mouth slackening. "Oh, I'm sorry. I guess I didn't think." Tears abruptly rimmed her eyes.

"No harm done," Fargo said, hoping he was right, and placed a hand on her shoulder. "You were just trying to be helpful."

She managed a wan grin. "I'm more trouble than I'm worth, aren't I?"

"I wouldn't say that."

"Only because you're a kind man. I'm sorry, Mr. Fargo. I'll try to be more observant in the future."

"Call me Skye," he said, glad they were finally on friendly terms. "I'll gather some wood outside that doesn't put off much smoke. You can still cook our meal." He went out and noticed Rosemary regarding him thoughtfully.

With the horses settled in, the next order of business was to drag the two station employees into the brush, dig shallow graves, and cover the bodies with a mound of stones. He removed everything from their pockets first. At the next station he would turn over their effects to the station keeper.

A fiery crescent rimmed the western horizon by the time he completed the burials and the wood gathering. He made a complete circuit of the station before going in, then put the items he'd taken from the dead men in his saddlebags.

"What do you think?" Rosemary asked.

The women had done a fine job of clearing the floor and making the station livable. Rosemary turned with a can in each hand and said, "All we found were these beans."

"And I have some jerky," Skye said. "It will have to do us until we get to Simpson's Park."

"You could shoot a rabbit or two," Lida said, and then did a double take as if she couldn't believe her own ears. "Listen to silly me! The Indians would hear the shots and know right where to find us."

"You're learning," Fargo said. He retrieved the jerky while Rosemary cooked the beans. The tantalizing aroma made his mouth water in anticipation. As much as he liked living off the land, he missed having a proper cooked meal every so often to break the routine.

He found a tin of nails and used the blunt end of a broken hatchet to tack lengths of a torn blanket over the windows. Only then did he light a lantern and place it on a table in the very center of the floor. Between the lantern and the stove, the station acquired a homey atmosphere that helped relieve the tension spawned by their frantic day.

There were two smaller rooms off the main room, both containing beds that had been stripped of their bedding. The mattresses were still there, although a Paiute had taken a knife to one and slashed part of the stuffing out.

Sitting at the table, his mouth crammed with jerky, Fargo watched the women hungrily devour their beans. "You ladies can divide the sleeping accommodations as you want," he told them. "I'll stay out here all night."

Rosemary lowered her spoon. "We can share a bed. We've done it before. Why don't you take the other one?"

"Because I can't afford to become too comfortable. If I do and the Paiutes hit us, we won't stand a chance," Fargo responded, and added, "There are no windows in the bedrooms so you'll be safe."

"I still don't think it's fair."

"I'll get by," Fargo assured her. "And sleeping on the floor is no worse than sleeping on the ground, which I've done more times than I care to count."

"I want to thank you for all you've done for us," Rosemary said, her gaze drifting across his broad chest and shoulders. "We'll never be able to thank you enough."

"Just stay alive. That's all the thanks I need," Fargo said, and saw Lida give him an odd glance. He heaped beans onto his plate and dug in with relish, his ears attuned to the sounds outside, the whisper of the wind and the movement of the horses in the corral.

"What if the Paiutes have wiped out every station between here and California?" Rosemary speculated.

"I doubt they have," Fargo said to set their fears at rest, but secretly he'd been concerned about the same possibility. If every last station had been destroyed or abandoned, getting the women to safety became a formidable task.

He chewed and pondered. The countryside was swarming with angry Paiutes and they would keep the Express and stage trail under scrutiny as much as possible. It might be safer to leave the trail and cut overland, but in this dry country he would be hard-pressed to find drinkable water. Plus there was the question of food. He could get by for days on very little. The women would suffer terribly.

Lida finished eating first and took her plate to the counter. She busied herself washing the plate in a basin, humming as she worked. Her entire attitude had changed since they arrived at the station and she was much more composed.

"What I wouldn't give for a shot of whiskey," Rosemary commented, and licked her full lips.

"Ever been to San Francisco before?" Fargo inquired.

"No, but I've heard all about the city from friends who have worked there. I can't wait to see if everything they told me is true."

"I gather you didn't like Denver?"

"Oh, Denver itself is all right. The woman we worked for, though, was a regular bitch. I imagine by now she's fit to be tied," Rosemary said, and laughed.

"Why's that?"

"Because Lida and I put one over on her. We wanted to leave Denver in the worst way but we didn't have the stage fare. So I told Madame Bovary that we needed an advance, two weeks' worth, so we could send for a couple of girls who were interested in coming out to work for her. And she fell for it."

Fargo didn't inquire as to the nature of the work. He already knew, and he was mildly surprised the women had been so open with him. Some would have hid the fact. But Rosemary and Lida impressed him as being simple souls who didn't indulge in habitual deceit. Well, not often, anyway.

He'd known scores of such women during his varied travels around the country, women who had drifted off the farm or who came from poor families in the big cities and were lured into offering their bodies for cash in the hope of accumulating a stake they could use to secure a better future. Most took up the trade out of desperation. There was little else a woman could do since men held the majority of jobs and generally frowned on women who worked outside of the home. And a lone woman, a lonely woman thrown by a cruel fate on her own devices, was easy prey for the human vultures who prowled the streets of the cities seeking young, gullible lovelies.

"What are you thinking about?" Rosemary asked unexpectedly.

"Nothing much," Fargo shrugged, and stretched. "You ladies should hit the hay. I want to make an early start tomorrow."

"What about you?"

"I'll check the horses and turn in," Fargo said. He picked up the Sharps and went outside, pausing at the doorway to scan the stage yard before exiting quickly so as not to frame his silhouette in the doorway.

All was peaceful. Insects buzzed in the night, and far off a coyote yipped and was answered by another.

He strolled to the corral and the Ovaro pranced over. "Ate your fill?" he said softly, and scratched the stallion's wide chest and neck. The Ovaro placed its nose against his neck. "You'll need all of your strength tomorrow," he predicted. "Those mangy Paiutes aren't about to let us get away this easily."

Another circuit of the station confirmed they were temporarily safe. He doubted the Paiutes would attack at night. Most Indians disliked doing so because they felt the spirits of warriors slain after dark were fated to aimlessly wander the earth instead of ascending to the Indian version of heaven. He didn't know if the Paiutes held to that belief, but the Apaches to the south definitely did. Which had always confounded him. The Apaches were fierce fighters, perhaps the best of any Indian tribe anywhere. They were afraid of no man but fearful of sorcery, ghosts, and witchcraft. They were a deathly superstitious lot, and a savvy man fighting an Apache band could always use their superstitions against them.

Fargo gazed at the stars for a while before entering the station on silent feet and closing the door behind him. One of the women had turned the lantern low but there was enough light for him to see. He took his bedroll and arranged it to the right of the door, then pulled the latch string inside so that no one could open the door from without. The only way for the Paiutes to get in would be to batter the door down, and at the first sound he would be up and ready with his rifle.

He stretched out on his back and cupped his hands behind his head. Despite his need for sleep, his mind wouldn't let him. He reviewed everything that had happened and projected a mental map of the region on the ceiling and tried to figure a way of reaching California without the risk of encountering the Paiutes.

Swinging north would be pointless. They'd have to cross blistering desert country and would drift into California east of Mount Shasta, a rugged land of steep canyons and lava beds that would make their horses go lame in no time. That was also Modoc territory, and the Modocs disliked the whites almost as much as the Paiutes. If the government wasn't careful, there would come a day when the Modocs went on the warpath, too.

Swinging south would be no better. After traversing miles and miles of arid land, they would have to contend with the Sierra Nevada range, which could be crossed safely only at a few known passes. The women lacked the proper clothes for riding at high elevations, and their food situation would be critical most of the way. Once over, they would be nearer Los Angeles than San Francisco.

So those two options were out of the question. And since they were closer to California than to Salt Lake City, so was going back. The more he pondered, the more convinced he became that their wisest course of action was to continue westward.

A soft rustling noise drew Skye's head around, and his breath caught in his throat at the sight of Rosemary Griffin in silken underclothes so sheer he could see every contour of her body.

# 6

A sly smile curved Rosemary's rosy lips as she boldly sashayed up to the spread bedroll and took a seat. The flimsy fabric covering her voluptuous body from her slender shoulders to her shapely thighs clung to her skin, accenting her creamy complexion and the inviting mound at the juncture of her legs.

Skye Fargo rose on his elbows, his mouth abruptly dry. His gaze glued to the twin peaks thrusting against her garment and he felt a stirring in his loins.

"I couldn't sleep," Rosemary said.

"I'm having a hard time getting to sleep myself."

"Lida is out to the world. She was exhausted. The poor dear just couldn't handle the nightmare we've been through."

"You're handling it well," Fargo said, watching her run an idle hand across her stomach. His manhood became granite hard.

Rosemary shrugged. "I learned long ago not to worry myself to death over things I can't control." She glanced at the stove, her lovely features highlighted by the lantern's dim glow. "I need my sleep, though, and there's one thing that always relaxes me enough so I can doze right off."

"What might that be?" Fargo responded, knowing full well what the answer was before he posed the question. So he wasn't the least bit surprised when she adopted a seductive smirk and leaned over to kiss him lightly on the mouth. Her lips were soft and warm and her breath, strangely enough, had the fragrance of mint.

He opened his mouth to dart out his tongue but she slid hers out first. Slick and moist, her tongue executed small circles around the tip of his. She placed her hands on his chest and melted flush against him.

In the back of Fargo's mind a tiny but insistent voice told him he should be getting badly needed sleep. But his body, on the verge of being fully aroused by her hands and her tongue and the exquisite feel of her breasts against his shirt, pulsed with quickened blood as well as desire. If she were to get up and leave at that minute, he wouldn't have been able to sleep for hours. So he opted to make the best of the situation.

His hands ran through her luxurious hair, then he gently caressed her neck with his fingertips. She squirmed delectably and shifted her mouth to his right ear where she nibbled on the lobe and breathed heavily.

In a deft motion Fargo rolled onto his left side, flipping her onto her back in the bargain, and licked the soft skin under her chin. Her right leg, slightly bent, swayed back and forth, rubbing his upper arm. About to turn his attention lower, he paused when he thought he heard a shuffling noise from across the room.

Rosemary saw him look up and tensed. "What is it? Something outside?"

"No," Skye replied. "I heard a noise from the bedroom. Are you sure Lida is sound asleep?"

"Of course I'm sure," Rosemary said, relaxing again and grinning. "She was sleeping like a baby when I came out here. Do you think I'd be doing this if she wasn't?" She put both hands on his cheeks and turned his face toward hers. "Now forget about her and finish what you've started."

What *I've* started? Fargo reflected wryly, but didn't debate the point. He cupped both breasts and massaged them, the sheer material tingling his palms, her nipples hardening rapidly under his knowing manipulation.

Their lips locked again, their tongues meshed, and Fargo roved his left hand down over her body, across her flat stomach to the silken juncture of her thighs, then almost to her knees before retracing his path to her breast.

Rosemary wiggled and moaned, her eyes closed, her expression dreamy. Her knee stroked his hip.

All Skye had to do was lift her underwear a fraction and his hand was on her hot pubic mound. Her whole body generated heat, but none so intense as at her slit.

He slid his middle finger over her nether lips and felt his hand grow slick with her flowing juices.

"Ohhhh!" Rosemary said, keeping her voice low.

He dipped his finger into her womanhood and she arched her back and dug her nails into his arms. She was so wet his hand dripped, and her inner walls closed around his finger with the fit of a glove.

"MMMmmmmm. I knew you'd know what to do," Rosemary said, smiling languidly.

Exposing her gorgeous globes, he swooped to her right breast and tongued the nipple while pumping his finger in and almost out of her passion-drenched tunnel. She humped her buttocks, rising to meet each thrust of his finger, and groaned loudly.

How long he kept at it, he couldn't say. Eventually, she yanked his lips from her breasts and looked him straight in the eye.

"I want you. I want you now."

Fargo didn't say a word. He pulled her underclothes off, then traced a path with his tongue down one side of her body and up the other. Cooing happily, she twisted from side to side, her skin breaking out in goose bumps. His finger stayed put in her womanhood and continued to plunge in and out.

Again he thought he heard a soft shuffling sound, but this time he didn't look up. It couldn't be Indians. If it came from the bedroom, then Lida must be awake. And he didn't care whether she was up or not. He wasn't about to stop for anything short of an all-out attack on the station.

At last, when Rosemary was pleading in a husky whisper for him to get on with it, he drew back and hastily removed his boots, gunbelt, and pants. Leaving his shirt and hat on, he grasped her hips and held her steady while he positioned his rigid pole at the entrance to heaven.

"Goodness!" Rosemary said, watching him expectantly. "I had no idea you were so big. I'll feel that clear up to my throat."

"You think so?" Skye said, grinning, and rammed his organ to the hilt without a hint of warning. She gasped, her back leaving the floor, her fingernails knifing into his shoulders, her eyes wide in disbelief. Great breaths came from her parted lips and her stomach heaved.

"Oh, God!" she wailed.

And Fargo let her have it, banging into her with the intensity of a rutting ram, holding her hips securely so she would experience each stroke to its full extent. She clung to him, her eyes closed once more, panting in rhythm to his movements, sounding like a steam engine about to blow a piston.

The lantern light danced over their rippling forms, throwing long shadows on the wall, shadows that writhed and bucked like a berserk snake. Perspiration caked their bodies, and the only sound was the slap-slap-slap of their abdomens and the occasional whines Rosemary uttered.

He rode her as he would a fine horse, pacing himself, holding himself in until just the right moment. Her arms were looped around his neck and she was shuddering intensely when he released her hips and pounded into her with a vengeance born of the explosion building at the base of his manhood.

"I'm coming!" she cried, apparently oblivious to being overheard by Lida. "Oh! I'm coming!"

So did Skye, his hands on the floor, his back bending upward as his face flushed crimson with the rush of fiery blood. He spurted, plunging into her as if he would break her apart, and she met every thrust with equal force while venting inarticulate cries.

Afterward, after he was spent and lying by her side, she tenderly stroked his cheek and said, "Thank you."

"Don't mention it."

"Anytime you want seconds, let me know."

"I'll keep the invitation in mind," Fargo promised, and touched her stomach. Her flesh quivered. Yet another noise to his rear made him roll onto his back just in time to see Lida's bedroom door close. She must have observed their coupling. Perhaps she had been watching the entire time.

"Something wrong?" Rosemary asked.

"No," Fargo said, propping an arm under his head. He felt totally at ease and knew he'd have no problem falling asleep now. Rosemary kissed his shoulder, and he was about to hug her when one of the horses whinnied. Instantly he sat up and began getting dressed.

"What's the matter?" Rosemary inquired, rising on an elbow.

"That was my stallion."

"Horses whinny all the time. It might not mean a thing."

"I know that stallion better than I know myself. Something—or someone—is out there," Fargo stated. He strapped on the Colt, then loosened the Arkansas toothpick in its slim sheath attached to his leg above the ankle. During their lovemaking he hadn't bothered to remove it. Given their predicament, he never knew when he might need a weapon at a moment's notice.

"You're going out there alone at this time of night?"

"I have to," Fargo said, drawing his Colt and spinning the cylinder. Five chambers were filled and there was an empty under the hammer. He stuck a shell in there, too. If the Paiutes were prowling around the station, he would need the extra round.

Rosemary rose to her knees and swiftly began donning her undergarments. "What can I do?"

"Keep the door bolted. I'll leave the Sharps and you also have the shotgun, so you should be able to hold them off if they get past me."

Rising, Rosemary gripped his left wrist. "Be careful, Skye. Please."

"Always," he assured her, and went to the lantern to kill the light completely. Then he moved to the door, worked the latch, and quickly slid out into the cool night, crouching as he stepped to the right so he wouldn't be silhouetted against the front of the building. Immediately the door was closed and he heard the bolt thrown.

Since the Paiutes were bound to be watching the station if they were in the vicinity, he invited a bullet or an arrow by staying close to the wall. Holding the Colt in his right hand, he eased onto his elbows and knees and crawled toward the corral.

Both Indian ponies were resting on the south side. The Ovaro, however, was erect and staring intently at a cluster of brush to the east of the corral.

What did it see or had it seen? Fargo wondered, crawling until he was next to the bottom rail. If not the Paiutes, then possibly a hungry mountain lion. Every sense alert, he slid toward the brush. Nothing moved. No unusual sounds reached his ears.

The stallion saw him and pawed the ground with a great hoof, then shook its head and snorted.

Fatigue pervaded Fargo's every pore. The fight and the long chase and the lovemaking had all taken their toll on his weary body, and he would have given anything to be able to curl up under a blanket and sleep for a week.

He gave his head a shake to disrupt his thoughts. Thinking about sleep at such a time could lose him his hair. He must be careful, extremely careful, and always alert.

For minutes that stretched indefinitely he lay there under the corral fence and waited for something to happen. The night remained tranquil, the breeze fluttering the leaves and sighing off across the vast plain. Lulled by the peace and quiet, his eyes drooped and his head bobbed.

With a start, he roused himself and blinked, annoyed at his lapse. Despite his best efforts, he might well doze off. He should keep moving to keep fully awake, so he crawled closer to the vegetation.

For all he knew, he might be wasting his time. The Ovaro had calmed down, and whatever had been out there might well be gone. He decided to go into the brush and check, and if he found no sign of man or beast he would return to the station for some badly needed rest.

A mesquite reared above him, and to his right were several boojum trees. There were varieties of cactus and yucca plants. Nowhere did he detect motion or see an incongruous dark form. Evidently the nocturnal visitor was gone.

Skye raised his head for a last look, about to shove to his feet, when the pad of rushing feet proved his assumption totally wrong. A heavy body landed square on his back, forcing the breath to whoosh from his lungs, and knees gouged into the base of his spine. He twisted his head to look over his shoulder and inadvertently saved his life.

A silvery blade streaked from overhead and thudded into the ground less than an inch from his cheek. He glimpsed the swarthy features of a sun-bronzed Paiute, and then he pushed off the ground and rolled.

The Paiute, unable to retain his balance, threw himself in the opposite direction, tugging his knife free as he did. With pantherish grace he rolled on his wide shoulders and surged erect, the knife held level at waist height, then he leaped.

A shade slower, Fargo tried to sidestep the brave and employ his Colt. But the Paiute slammed into him in a diving tackle and they went down. Fargo was suddenly on his back, the Paiute on top, his hand locked on the Paiute's knife arm while the Indian's hand held his right wrist to prevent him from pointing the Colt.

In grim combat they strained, each striving to gain the advantage, the brave hissing through clenched teeth. Fargo shifted and squirmed to get out from under the powerful warrior and succeeding in getting a leg in the clear. In a flash he drove his knee into the Paiute's ribs, not once but three times, each blow delivered harder than the one before, and on the third sweep the Paiute flinched, tore himself loose, and stood.

Skye brought the gun up and out. His thumb was curling on the hammer when the Paiute's foot flicked out, numbing his wrist and sending the Colt sailing. Defenseless, he scrambled backward as the Paiute swung the knife at his neck and missed. He uncoiled like a steel spring, his hand whipping past his ankle sheath when he straightened, the toothpick shimmering in the subdued light.

The Paiute stopped, warily regarding the slender knife. He crouched, his left arm held diagonally across his stout body to ward off strikes at his face and stomach while his right hand jabbed with his weapon.

Fargo had been in enough knife fights to know the warrior was skilled and supremely deadly. He parried, thrust, and narrowly evaded a swing that would have slit his throat from ear to ear. As he fought, he kept expecting to hear other warriors rush toward him or to feel the sharp pang of an arrow penetrating his back. He couldn't believe the Paiute was alone, and he wanted to end their conflict swiftly before reinforcements arrived.

Slashing and shifting, stabbing and ducking, they fought on. Constantly they circled one another, changing position again and again. On one such occasion Fargo spied a knee-high cactus directly behind the unsuspecting

Paiute. He couldn't tell what kind of cactus it was in the dark, but a cactus wouldn't be a cactus if it didn't have some sort of pointed barbs or thorns capable of rending human flesh as easily as the best butcher or bowie knife ever made.

So it was that Skye suddenly lunged straight out, and predictably the Paiute danced straight backward. Straight into the cactus. There was the rough scraping of a moccasin against the wicked barbs, and the Paiute glanced down, distracted by the pain for the blink of an eye. In that interval Fargo lunged again, only this time he scored, the Arkansas toothpick slicing into the warrior all the way to the hilt.

Gasping, the Paiute stiffened and gaped at the toothpick. Then he rallied and swung once more, determined to sell his life as dearly as he could.

Fargo's fingers slipped off the hilt as he darted to the left. The brave's knife ripped into his sleeve, nicking the skin and drawing a trickle of blood. Backpedaling, he dodged other swings, each increasingly reckless. The Paiute's strength was fading fast and the warrior wanted to finish the job before becoming too weak to fight.

Of all times, Skye tripped. His ankle hit an exposed root or a low limb and down he went. The Paiute closed in, the knife already descending. Skye rammed his legs into the warrior's kneecap, heard the distinct crack that stopped the brave in his tracks, and rolled to the left.

The Paiute crumpled. Slowly, twisting in a spiral, one hand on the toothpick and the other feebly holding his own knife, the warrior sank to the ground, trembled convulsively, and died.

Fargo had no time to take a breather. He squatted, his senses probing the night, seeking other braves. In the corral one of the horses munched and crunched. To the west a coyote howled. No one stirred near the station. Could it be that the warrior had been alone? Perhaps the Paiutes had sent out scouts to try and find where he and the women were holed up. Perhaps this had been a lone warrior who had seen the horses and intended to steal them. He didn't know. To play it safe he wrenched the toothpick out and wiped the blade clean on the dead warrior's breechclout. Then he located the Colt, squatted behind a bush, and listened for a full five minutes before being completely convinced there were no more braves.

Six-shooter in hand, Fargo conducted a thorough search of the property bordering the station. Once he inadvertently spooked a rabbit from out of a thicket, but otherwise he encountered no other living thing and certainly no more Paiutes.

At the door he stopped to think. He doubted the Paiute had been on foot but he wasn't about to go any great distance from the building to find the mount. Then again, maybe the brave had been left afoot for some reason and that explained why he was after the horses. Either way, there might be other Paiutes who would show up looking for their fellow. He had to be long gone with the women when the others arrived.

Rosemary opened the door quickly after he knocked and announced himself, her features creasing in heartfelt relief when he entered. She saw fresh dirt on his buckskins, the tear in his sleeve, and a bloody smudge on his chin. "What happened?" she asked in alarm.

"A Paiute and I went a few rounds," Fargo answered, locking the door behind him.

"Let me see that arm."

"It's nothing. A scratch," Fargo told her, stepping to a chair and taking a seat.

"It still can use tending," Rosemary persisted, and examined the nick carefully. "You're right. But you've bled some. I'll get a cloth and clean the wound."

The brush of naked feet on the floor made Fargo twist around. He barely suppressed his reaction at seeing Lida shuffling toward them, attired in her underclothes just like Rosemary. Nothing was left to the imagination.

"What's going on?" she inquired, sleepily rubbing her eyes. "What's all the discussion about?"

Fargo knew she couldn't have been asleep for very long, if at all, and he suspected her act was a sham to convince him she had been sleeping the whole time he and Rosemary had been making love. He couldn't help but notice Lida's body was alluring in its own right. Her breasts were smaller, but pert, and through her underwear could be glimpsed the profuse dark thatch covering her pubic mound. Those long, slender legs of hers started a train of thought better left until he was well rested.

"Skye killed a Paiute," Rosemary said.

All pretense at being sleepy evaporated faster than the morning dew under a blistering sun, and Lida came to the table and stared at Fargo's wound. "Are you all right?"

"Fine, thanks."

Lida glanced at the door and licked her lips. "Are there more out there? Are we about to be attacked?"

"I don't think so."

"Do we stay put or leave?" Lida asked.

"We'll stick to our original plan and sleep here until morning," Fargo said.

"I'd rather head for the next station."

"So would I," Fargo agreed. "But the horses come first, and they need their rest if they're to be of any use tomorrow." He motioned toward her bedroom. "So why don't you lay back down and try to get some shut-eye?"

"I'll try, but I'm not making any promises," Lida said. She walked a few yards, then grinned at him. "Please try to keep the noise down. I swear I thought I heard a wrestling match going on out here earlier." Chuckling, she retired.

Skye glanced at Rosemary, who made a point of avoiding his gaze. He sat in silence while she administered to the cut, wondering what kind of game the two women were playing.

"There," Rosemary said when she was done. She placed the cloth and the pan of water on the counter. "Now I think I'll turn in, too, unless you have other ideas?"

The blatant invitation amused him. "Another time, perhaps. I need my sleep."

"If you insist," Rosemary pouted, and gave him a lingering kiss full on the lips before she walked off, her hips swaying with an invitation of their own.

Taking the Sharps, Fargo took up his post by the door, reclining on his back on his blankets. If all went well—which was highly unlikely—they should reach Simpson's Park before noon. He wasn't quite as eager to get the women off his hands, but he did want to reach safety as soon as possible. No matter how clever he was, he couldn't hope to keep the Paiutes at bay indefinitely. There were simply too many.

Counting on his internal clock to awaken him on time, he closed his eyes and let the tension drain from his body. Normally, he awakened shortly before dawn, so they could be on their horses and on the road before the sun even rose. The last images in his brain before slumber claimed him were of Rosemary and Lida, standing stark naked side by side and beckoning him to them with sensual smiles.

He grinned in his sleep.

# 7

Skye Fargo knew something was terribly wrong the instant his eyes flicked wide. He sat up, taking stock, aware the room was much hotter than it should be at daybreak. Rising, he swung the door open and halted in consternation.

The day was hours old.

He'd overslept! Stunned, he ran out, squinting in the harsh sunlight. The horses were standing near the water trough, and the Ovaro saw him and bobbed its head as if in impatient demand for its breakfast. Retracing his steps, he cupped his hands to his mouth and shouted, "Get up and get dressed! We've overslept." Then he went out and hastily fed their animals from the bin.

The lethargic flapping of large wings caused him to swing around. Several vultures had found the dead Paiute and were eating greedily. Far overheard soared others, circling in to join the feast.

Fargo swore, knowing the Paiutes would spy those buzzards and come to investigate. When he went inside both women were dressed and fussing with their hair. "We have to ride," he announced.

"Do we have time to eat?" Rosemary asked him. "There are a few beans left over from last night."

"No," Fargo answered. "Every minute we spend here increases the risk of being found."

Lida opened her mouth as if to protest, then apparently thought better of the notion.

It took two minutes for Fargo to saddle the Ovaro and tie down the *mochila*. Since he wanted to avoid the rutted ribbon constituting the stage and Express road at all costs, he pushed southeastward, intending to make a loop and come up on Simpson's Park from the south.

He held the horses to a brisk walk, saving them for

when they would really be needed. They hadn't gone a quarter of a mile when he and the Ovaro were caked with sweat. His canteen was full, but the water wouldn't last them long in such heat and he hunted for sign of a tank or a spring. There were no rivers or streams for the next twenty-five miles or more.

The women said little. They realized the gravity of the situation and rode alertly.

"Look!" Lida exclaimed as they topped out on a dry wash, and pointed to the northeast.

A large dust cloud swirled like a thing alive.

"The Paiutes," Fargo said. "They've found the dead brave at the station and they're after us."

"Oh, no," Lida groaned.

Now Skye went due east, sighting on a distant butte. He rode faster reluctantly, knowing how hard it would be on the horses. But he didn't break into a full gallop yet. The dust raised would tell the Paiutes exactly where to find them. Without it, the Paiutes were forced to follow their tracks, a much slower process.

The air was deathly still. There were no sounds other than the drumming of hoofs and the creak of saddle leather. Not so much as a lizard moved on the sun-baked landscape.

"How could anyone live in such a land?" Rosemary mused aloud.

"The Paiutes have been in this region for generations," Fargo explained. "Some say they were driven here by stronger tribes and forced to make the best of it. They've always been a poor tribe, because the land is so poor, but they're hard like the land, too. They've adapted well. They know where to go at particular times of the year to find game and edible plants and nuts." He paused. "They made do until the past couple of years when the white man came in and upset the apple cart by taking valuable food away from them."

"You certainly can't blame the whites for the atrocities the Paiutes have committed," Lida said.

"There's blame on both sides," Fargo said. "If you had a dollar for every time our government has lied to the Indians, you'd never have to work again."

"There are those who say all Indians should be exterminated," Lida commented.

Fargo knew all about the bigots. He'd met plenty. And he knew that many prominent politicians and influential newspaper editors were trying to stir up the American people against all Indians, claiming it was the God-given right of the white race to conquer or destroy those "heathens" who refused to become forcibly civilized.

Having lived among the Sioux and other tribes, Fargo knew Indians for what they really were. Not savages, although when on the warpath they showed no mercy to male or female, young or old. Not heathens, because every tribe practiced its own special religion and all of them believed in the existence of a Great Mystery or Great Spirit, as it was more commonly known. And they definitely didn't deserve extermination, because Indians were people, pure and simple, people who shared the same hopes and aspirations of their white enemies.

Both were interested in rearing families and being successful members of their communities. Both liked to acquire what luxuries they could. Where a white man might want a sturdy house, an Indian preferred a comfortable lodge or wickiup. Where a white man craved money in the bank, an Indian craved a herd of fine horses. A white man went for fancy suits, an Indian for the best buckskins and blankets he could obtain.

There were more similarities than there were differences, and Fargo felt it was a damned shame the two races would never be able to live in peace. As it was, he had become one of the unique few who could live in either world, white or red, and do so with ease. Most of the best scouts and trackers had spent time among the Indians and adopted many Indian ways. Men such as Kit Carson, Jim Bridger, Daniel Boone, and others all owed their celebrated status to the lessons they had learned from their Indian brothers. And, truth to tell, so did he.

The butte reared above them before long, and Skye skirted along its base to the north. He studied the sheer walls, seeking a place where he could climb.

"What are you looking for?" Rosemary asked.

Skye told her.

"Why?"

"I figure I can hold off the war party with my Sharps long enough for you ladies to ride to Simpson's Park."

"Leave us to fend for ourselves?" Lida exclaimed, and

vigorously shook her head. "Not on your life, mister. I feel a hell of a lot safer with you by my side."

"I feel the same way," Rosemary said.

"You can make it if you ride slow so you don't raise any dust," Fargo said. "The Paiutes will think all of us are here at the butte."

"And what if there are more Paiutes between here and the station?" Rosemary brought up. "What chance would we have then?"

"Please stay with us," Lida pleaded.

There was no way of getting around it. Fargo thought his plan would work, but he couldn't make the women go if they refused. "All right," he said gruffly. "Just don't blame me if the Paiutes catch us sooner or later." He jerked on the reins and cut due north, trying to estimate exactly where the station would be.

A stretch of rock-hard ground unfolded before them, and Fargo increased the pace. Not only wouldn't they create dust, but they'd leave few hoofprints and the war party would go even slower. Although, when he reflected further, he realized the Paiutes would soon guess their destination and no longer have to rely on tracking.

He kept hoping to espy a column of smoke from the station chimney, but the horizon was clear and blue, not so much as a cloud marring the sky. That is, until they had ridden several miles and a few black dots materialized, small dots that gradually grew bigger and acquired the shape of circling birds. Big, black circling birds.

Buzzards.

"Are those what I think they are?" Lida inquired.

"Yes," Fargo grimly assured her.

"Son of a bitch!"

They found the station without difficulty, or what was left of it. Simpson's Park had been burned to the ground and only a jumble of black timbers remained. The corral had been torn down, the stock taken. Nearby lay the mutilated body of the station keeper.

"Oh, God," Lida breathed in horror, and turned her head from the corpse.

"We should bury the poor bastard," Rosemary said.

"No time," Fargo responded, then checked the vicinity for a spring. There was none, nor was there a water tank here. The trough was empty, a hole about the size of the

*64*

tip of a stout lance in the wood at the bottom. Without delay he rode westward, staying with the Express route to make better time. The women rode on either side.

"What now?" Lida asked.

"What else? We ride to the next station and hope to hell it's still standing."

"What is it called?"

Fargo had to think a bit before he could remember the name.

"Reese River Station."

"Then there will be water there!" Lida exclaimed.

"Maybe not," Fargo said. "Most of the rivers in this territory only flow during the wet season." He didn't aggravate her anxiety by mentioning that they must find water by nightfall or come tomorrow their horses would be worn to a frazzle and they'd be easily overhauled by the first war party that came on their trail.

They pushed onward in somber silence. Every so often a sluggish hint of a breeze caressed their brows. Otherwise, the air hung dry and hot.

Four miles from the station Fargo cut to the north and slowed down. They had probably gained a little ground on the Paiutes, and now he intended to make their tracks as difficult to read as he could. To that end, he stuck to the hardest ground he could find, often riding over tracts of solid rock. And he never rode in a straight line for more than a few hundred yards. By repeatedly slanting to the right and left, he hoped to confuse the war party.

They were nearing a series of low hills when Fargo saw a brilliant pinpoint of light shimmer for several seconds on a flat crowned hill directly ahead. Keeping his voice level, he warned the women. "Don't look up or act afraid. There's someone on top of the hill in front of us."

"How do you know?" Rosemary asked.

"I saw a reflection," Fargo said. He spotted a gully on the south side of the hill. It would give him some cover almost to the rim. Acting nonchalant and natural, he placed his right hand on the butt of his Colt. "I'm going up this gully," he let them know. "When I make my move, put your heels in those ponies and go a mile or so. If I don't catch up in half an hour, you'll be on your own."

"We're not leaving you," Rosemary responded.

"Don't be stubborn. There could be Paiutes up there."

"So you'd sacrifice your life to let us get away," Rosemary said, and shook her head. "No matter what else we might be, we're not cowards. We'll stick by you, Skye, come what may."

Annoyed, Fargo glared at her but she refused to meet his gaze. Since they were almost to the gully he couldn't very well waste time arguing. "All right. But stay at the bottom of the gully until I let you know it's safe."

"Please be careful," Lida cautioned.

He nodded, then came even with the mouth of the gully. Simultaneously, he hauled on the reins and dug his spurs into the Ovaro's flanks. The stallion jumped into a gallop and took off up the gully with its hoofs clattering on the stones covering the bottom. Whoever was up there would hear the noise, which couldn't be helped. Fargo had to reach the top quickly, before any hidden riflemen picked him off.

The gully ended a dozen yards shy of the crest and he banked sharply to the left, where the soil was softer and would muffle the Ovaro's hoofs. Colt in hand, he cleared the rim and swung toward the first and only figures he saw, two men caught flat-footed with nothing in their hands but a pair of field glasses.

"Don't shoot, mister!" cried the smaller of the two. "We're white and we're friendly!"

Skye held the Colt low and steady. White they were, but the West crawled with killers, thieves, and hard cases of every sort. Outlaw bands in every state and territory made life miserable for decent farmers and ranchers. In the cities it was worse; a man didn't dare walk down certain dark alleys at certain times for fear of having a gun or knife shoved in his back and his money stolen. The simple fact was that a person couldn't afford to be too trusting toward strangers, and these two had deceit written all over them.

The speaker was a thin, older man in Levis and a brown shirt streaked with dirt and food stains. His pointed chin was covered by grizzled stubble. Crafty green eyes took their measure of Fargo and narrowed warily.

His companion stood well over six feet and possessed

wide shoulders and a broad chest. He wore a buckskin shirt, black pants, and a flat-brimmed black hat. His mane of hair was black, his eyes a deep brown.

Both men wore revolvers on their right hips and the larger man had a bowie in a sheath on his left side.

"We sure were surprised to see you," said the talkative one. "Thought you might be Injuns until we got a good look at you."

Fargo noticed the field glasses they held were expensive models in fine condition, a stark contrast to their worn, dirty clothes and old saddles, leading him to wonder if the field glasses hadn't been stolen. "Who are you and what are you doing here?"

The big one squared his shoulders and spoke harshly. "I don't like your tone of voice, *hombre*."

"Tough. Answer the question."

Both men exchanged glances, then the smaller one smiled and took a half step forward. "Listen, mister. There's no call for you to brace us this way, especially since I imagine you're in the same trouble we are. We want to reach California with our body parts still in one piece, and I reckon you want to do the same."

"Keep talking," Fargo directed.

"Well, my name is Pete Howard and this here is Rafe Slade. We were on our way from Salt Lake City to San Francisco when all hell broke loose."

Fargo said nothing, his face inscrutable. But he had heard of Rafe Slade, and nothing he had heard would make the man welcome in polite society.

"The Paiutes are all over this area and we've been lucky avoiding them so far," Howard said. "We're low on grub, though, and our canteens are about empty." He paused. "You wouldn't happen to have any you could share?"

"No."

"What about those women you're with?" Slade asked gruffly.

An instinctive dislike for the man almost compelled Fargo to move closer and knock him senseless with the Colt. He restrained his temper with an effort. "They don't have any supplies at all. And we need water as badly as you do."

"Rafe claims there's a tank close by here, but we haven't been able to find it," Howard revealed.

"I don't claim nothing," Slade snapped. "A stage driver told me about it back in a card game in Salt Lake."

Howard gestured at the Colt in Fargo's hand. "There's no reason for you to keep pointing that six-shooter at us unless you aim to use it."

Without saying a word, Fargo twirled the revolver into his holster and pondered his options. As much as he would like extra company and extra guns to help protect the women, he didn't rate these two as reliable traveling companions. He'd rather they went their own way. But before he could make his feelings known, the thud of hoofs on the slope heralded the arrival of Rosemary and Lida.

"Well, lookee here!" Howard declared, smirking.

Slade's eyes lit up like those of a wolf that had found two juicy lambs.

Fargo turned the stallion so he could keep an eye on them and gave the women a stern look of disapproval. "I thought I told you to stay below."

"We didn't hear any shooting so we figured it was safe," Rosemary said, drawing rein. She regarded Howard and Slade for a moment. "I'm sorry. We should have listened to you."

Lida was all smiles. "Hello, gentlemen," she greeted them. "You don't know how relieved we are to find you. We're trying to reach California and we'd be grateful if you could help us get there."

"You don't need to twist my arm," Howard said, and cackled.

"Teaming up with us is a smart idea," Slade said. "With us along you won't need to fret your pretty heads over the mangy Paiutes."

"Then it's settled," Lida declared, sounding vastly relieved. "We'll ride together."

"I don't know—," Rosemary said uncertainly.

Lida shot her a quizzical glance. "What's wrong?"

"Yeah, lady," Slade added, his features clouding with barely suppressed anger. "What's the matter?"

Fargo resented the hard case's attitude and promptly

came to Rosemary's rescue. "We don't need the two of you," he said. "You go your way and we'll go ours."

"But that makes no sense," Pete Howard replied. "This country is crawling with Paiutes. Together, we have a chance of reaching Californy alive." He appealed to Lida. "What harm can it do? And wouldn't you feel safer with our guns to help protect you ladies?"

Lida didn't need any convincing. She turned on Skye. "I don't understand. Why don't you want them to go along?"

"I'm sure Skye has his reasons," Rosemary said.

"Skye?" Slade blurted. His right hand, which had been hooked in his belt above his six-shooter, discreetly moved away from the gun and closer to his large silver buckle. He raked the Trailsman from head to toe with a probing gaze. "You wouldn't happen to be Skye Fargo, would you?"

Fargo simply nodded.

"I'll be damned," Pete Howard breathed, and took a half step backward. "Listen, Mr. Fargo, we don't want no trouble with the likes of you. But we'd be in your debt if you'd let us tag along with you to the border."

Rosemary looked from one to the other, clearly puzzled. "Do you two gentlemen know Fargo?"

"Not personally," Howard responded. "But everyone in these parts has heard of him. Hell, everyone between the muddy Mississippi and the Pacific has heard tales of the Trailsman at one time or another. He's right up there with Carson and the like."

"The Trailsman?" Rosemary said. "Why, I've heard of him, too. They say he's killed a hundred men or better."

"Not counting Injuns," Howard said.

Rosemary stared at Skye as if seeing him for the very first time. "Are you really him? The Trailsman?"

"Some people call me by that handle," Fargo allowed.

Lida appeared unimpressed. "Even if you are as good as Kit Carson, it's no reason for you to turn down help when it's kindly offered. And you know we'll be safer riding with these two men. I say they're welcome to come if they want."

"What about you?" Fargo asked Rosemary.

She paused, then shrugged. "I really don't know. I

suppose it would be better to have them with us. The more guns we have, the safer we'll be, right?"

"Of course that's right," Lida said, and motioned for Howard and Slade to mount their horses. "What are you waiting for? We can't stay here forever."

Howard glanced at Fargo, and when no objection was forthcoming he chuckled and swung onto his dun. "Thanks for the invite, ladies. This has to be the best bit of luck we've had in a coon's age."

"Ain't that the truth," Slade said, and smacked his thick lips as if about to partake of a succulent feast.

# 8

For the next hour Fargo only spoke when addressed, and even then he limited himself to one- or two-word answers. After all he had done to help Rosemary and Lida, he keenly resented the fact they hadn't seen fit to heed his advice. He knew what was best for them and they ought to know it by now. But if they wanted to learn their lesson the hard way, that was all right with him.

He took the lead so he would be the first to spot any Paiutes lurking ahead, although he disliked having his back toward Howard and Slade. Either one was capable of plugging another person between the shoulder blades without a moment's hesitation or any remorse, but he figured neither would try anything while they were still in the heart of Paiute country knowing a shot would carry for miles.

Rosemary, he noticed, treated him differently since learning he was the Trailsman. Why, he didn't know. So far as he was aware, none of the stories circulating about him painted him as a bad character. But there was no mistaking her new aloof, cold attitude. Fine! he reflected. Let her act like an ass. And let both of them get what they had coming. He wasn't about to interfere. They were grown adults. They deserved what they got.

Skye paid little attention to the conversations behind him. Lida and Pete talked nonstop, with comments by Rosemary and Slade every so often. Howard had told them he'd been to San Francisco a few times and Lida was plying him for all the information she could glean.

"Where might you be headed, Fargo?" Howard asked when Lida finally ran out of questions.

"California," Fargo replied. He was leading them along the winding bottom of a serpentine draw. Whenever he could, he dropped below ground level to reduce the risk of being spotted by a passing war party.

"I mean where exactly?" Howard persisted.

Fargo looked at him. "I had no idea you worked for a newspaper."

"Me? One of those muley journalists?" Howard said, and laughed. "Why, I have trouble spelling my own name. I never had much schooling when I was younger."

Slade snorted. "You missed the point, idiot."

"Huh?"

"Fargo was telling you to mind your own business," Slade explained. "He knows you don't work for no paper."

"Oh," Howard said, and clammed up.

From Slade's appearance, Fargo would not have expected the man to catch on so quickly. Under all that bushy hair and behind those close-knit eyes was a sharp mind. He decided he had better not underestimate Rafe Slade again or he might live to regret it.

The draw ended and Fargo went up the left side, a gradual slope that brought him out amidst mesquite and sage. Halting, he scanned the plain beyond and tensed on seeing a dust cloud to the northwest. He could see several of the lead riders, and although they were too distant to note details he saw several of them moving an arm up and down as if slapping their mounts. Indians using quirts, he realized, and turned the pinto.

"What's wrong?" Rosemary asked.

"More Paiutes," Fargo replied. "Back down to the bottom of the draw. We'll wait until they're gone."

Once safely below, they waited expectantly, listening to the faint drumming of many hoofs, a drumming that grew ever louder.

"What if they find us?" Lida inquired anxiously.

"I doubt they saw me," Fargo said. "And unless they ride right up to the draw, they won't have any idea we're here."

Howard peered at the walls of earth on both sides. "I don't much cotton to being hemmed in. Give me open space where I can ride like hell and I'll have those Injuns eating my dust."

The pounding had become louder still.

"They're heading our way," Rafe Slade commented, his hand on his revolver.

Fargo had guessed the same thing. He estimated the war party wasn't more than one hundred yards off and riding ever closer. It wasn't the same band that had been trailing him and the women, so there was no reason to suspect the Paiutes had any idea there were whites within fifty miles.

And then the war party stopped.

Lida gasped, and Fargo glanced at her, ready to lunge and clamp a hand over her should she go to cry out. In the dry air the slightest sound would carry far and Indians possessed keen hearing. They had to, with their very survival often depending on the sharpness of their senses. Even more keen were the senses of Indian ponies, many former wild horses that had been caught and trained. What the Indian didn't hear, his mount often did.

No one dared move. No one so much as whispered. Into the draw wafted the murmur of a heated conversation.

Fargo figured two of the warriors were arguing, perhaps over which direction to take or which ranch or station to attack next. He fervently hoped the band would move on soon, and a minute later he broke into a grin when he heard them move out. But his grin changed to a frown the very next instant.

Rosemary's horse nickered. Not loudly, not long, but the harm was done.

There was an exclamation up above and the war party abruptly stopped. One of the Paiutes spoke, followed by the noise made by a single horse as it came closer and closer to the draw.

Skye drew his Colt. The brave was searching for the horse that had neighed, and once he spotted the draw they were in hot water. He listened to another exclamation, and the searcher shouted something to the rest of the band.

"We've got to hightail it!" Howard hissed.

Nodding, Fargo motioned for them to retrace their steps. Howard took the lead, wisely going slowly. Fargo held back, hoping the searcher would assume there were wild horses in the draw and nothing more.

Fresh sweat erupted along Fargo's brow, his palms became slick. He curled his thumb around the hammer. The crunch of hoofs was very near now, so near he swore he could hear the animal still breathing heavily after having been ridden so hard. He was surprised there were so many bands of mounted Paiutes abroad; from what he'd been told back in Salt Lake City, the Paiutes weren't rich in horses as were the Sioux and the Cheyennes.

Suddenly the warrior materialized, a bow with a nocked arrow held loosely in his left hand.

Their eyes met, and in the Paiute's flared hatred and resolve. He lifted his bow even as he started to shout.

Fargo squeezed off two swift shots, his slugs tearing into the brave's chest and flipping the man off his horse. Putting his spurs to the stallion, Fargo tore off after the others who were already in full flight. Strident yells broke out behind him and he knew the rest of the war party was closing in.

The ride down the draw was a nightmare made real. He never knew when Paiutes might appear on the rim and cut loose. Dust from the horses ahead obscured the bottom and got into his nose and eyes. He mentally reviewed the meandering course of the draw, trying to anticipate turns and switchbacks.

A buzzing arrow narrowly missed his right elbow.

One look showed him there were Paiutes strung out along the left rim. The foremost braves were armed with bows and lances. A few carrying rifles were farther back. One of those snapped off a shot and the bullet plucked at the crown of his hat.

He must do something before reaching the mouth of the draw. Once out on the plain the Paiutes would have clear shots and might be able to overtake and encircle his party's weary horses. If the Paiutes could be driven back, however momentarily, it would give Rosemary and Lida a chance to gain a substantial lead. He jammed the Colt into his holster and shucked the Sharps.

Skye made his move at a point where part of the left side of the draw had collapsed, leaving a natural ramp from bottom to top. He went up it on the fly, then yanked on the reins and wheeled the stallion.

Twenty-five yards off the lead Paiute lifted a bow.

Acting on pure reflex Fargo fed a bullet into the rifle, tucked the stock to his shoulder, and fired. His gun blasted at the same moment the shaft let fly. The warrior clutched at his forehead, then dropped, but Fargo didn't see him land because he twisted in pain when the arrow gouged a furrow in his left side. The shaft streaked past, trailing a fine crimson spray in its wake.

Since examining the wound would have to wait, Fargo slew the second Paiute in line with a shot to the head. Those behind broke and scattered, making for cover, a few going down into the draw. None were willing to contest the Sharps's superior range and accuracy.

It was astounding how quickly the warriors gained concealment. One minute there were nineteen onrushing braves; the next Fargo didn't have a target. He turned the stallion and galloped after his companions.

The harrowing race continued. Twice Fargo wheeled and fired, each time delaying the band for precious seconds. When at last he came to where the draw began, the women and the hard cases were two hundred yards or better to the east, fleeing rapidly. He followed, keeping his eyes on the left side of the draw and the furious Paiutes. The braves who had gone into the draw had not yet shown up. He believed his delaying tactic had been successful and before too long the women would be safe. Had a bullet not whizzed past his shoulder from the right, he never would have realized his mistake until it was too late.

Seven Paiutes were sweeping around the right end of the draw. They had somehow gained the right rim farther back, and they were much closer than the braves on the left side. By swinging wide, they were in a position to flank Fargo and maybe cut him off from the women, Slade, and Howard, and that was exactly the course they adopted. Simultaneously, the warriors on the left renewed their attack with vigor.

Fargo couldn't down them all. And with the two groups positioned like the pincers on a crayfish and about to catch him between them, he was forced to change direction. He bore to the right, his body low over the stallion. There were low hills and ravines to the south. If he could reach them, he might lose the Paiutes. It meant losing sight of Rosemary and Lida, but it couldn't be helped given the circumstances. He could always work his way back and pick up their trail later.

The two groups of braves came together. Words were shouted, and nine of them came on after Skye. The rest of the war party hastened eastward on their original course.

He scowled and rode on. If the women were captured, they could expect little mercy. Unlike some tribes, which adopted captive women and children, the Paiutes would slay Rosemary and Lida after first letting those warriors who wanted to indulge themselves do so. At least Slade and Howard would protect them, or so he hoped. Despite his dislike of the pair, he couldn't see them deserting the women. It would take the most miserable sort of son of a bitch imaginable to do such a thing, and while Slade and Howard had undoubtedly been living on the wrong side of the tracks for quite some time, neither impressed him as being so utterly cold-hearted they would abandon helpless women to the cruelest of fates.

Then again . . .

Eager to lose the pursuing Paiutes, Fargo rode into the hills. There were trees here, and enough underbrush to conceal him as he made his way into a narrow ravine. He was taking a risk, he knew. If there was no way out at the other end, the band would have him trapped. But if there was, he would come out above them and be able to discourage them with the Sharps.

To his dismay, the ravine narrowed more and more the farther he advanced. At length he was riding between two sheer walls, his stirrups brushing on either side. The stallion didn't like it one bit and kept jerking its head in impatience, anxious to be in the open.

If the passage should taper to a dead end, Fargo would be at the end of his rope. He would have to back the Ovaro out, a slow, time-consuming process that would bring him face-to-face with the Paiutes who would be gleefully waiting to turn him into a porcupine with their arrows and lances.

The cliffs pressed in closer, forcing Skye to loop his left leg over the saddle horn in order to continue. Minutes dragged by with awful slowness. He spied massive boulders perched above him and dreaded what would occur should one of them suddenly fall.

Just when it seemed as if there would be no end to the nerve-racking ordeal, the gap widened abruptly and he emerged in a grassy glen. On his ears fell the gurgle of flowing water, and relying on the Ovaro to find the source he let the pinto have its head and shortly drew rein before a circular pool fed by a sparkling downpour of the precious liquid, a downpour seeming to originate in the center of the cliff above.

Dismounting, Skye dropped to his hands and knees and swallowed a few refreshing mouthfuls. Then he stood, grabbed the Sharps, and left the stallion to drink at its leisure while he moved to the gap and pondered. Before too long the Paiutes would show up. From where he stood, he could easily keep them at bay.

Turning, he spied an ancient game trail leading from the pool in a winding course to the rim of the ravine. So he had a way out. The Ovaro was gulping water, parched from the blistering heat that scorched every pore. And there was grass for the pinto to eat. As much as Skye wanted to take off after Rosemary and Lida, common sense advised him to stay put for a while, to let the Ovaro eat and drink to its heart content. Then, when he did ride off, the stallion would be completely refreshed.

He leaned his back against the smooth wall, cradled the Sharps in the crook of his arm, and waited. He remembered how the passage had been fairly straight from start to finish, which sprouted the germ of an idea.

All he could do was wait.

The Ovaro had finished drinking and was chomping green grass when the dull thud of hoofs alerted Skye to the arrival of the band. Crouching, he gazed into the defile and glimpsed indistinct shapes moving toward him. Shrouded in the deep shadows at the bottom of the gloomy gap, the Paiutes were moving as stealthily as they could but the high walls amplified every noise.

Fargo knelt, pressed the Sharps to his shoulder, and waited until he could distinguish the lead brave. The warrior spotted him and shouted. Whatever the Paiute was saying became drowned out a second later by the booming of the rifle.

Magnified by the walls until the sharp retort of the shot resembled a clap of thunder, the echo reverberated back and forth. There were more yells and the panicked neighing of war ponies.

Fargo fired again, then once more.

A low rumble ensued, becoming gradually louder, until the rumble became a roar and the roar became a veritable din. For a few brief moments the ground trembled as if from an earthquake, and suddenly a tremendous cloud of dirt and dust billowed out of the gap.

Skye flattened as the roiling cloud swept over him. Wind buffeted his hat and stirred his hair. He held his face close to the ground, breathing shallowly, but still got stinging particles into his eyes and mouth. Coughing, he bent at the waist and covered his eyes with one hand. Dirt smacked against his cheeks and stung his back.

After a while the racket subsided, the cloud dispersed, and the last of the dust settled to the ground. Fargo slowly stood, coughed again, and stared in somber fascination at the defile. Tons of boulders and rocks now packed the gap from bottom to top. Evidently his shots had started some of the huge boulders rolling, and once in motion the unstoppable colossi had started a stone and rock avalanche that crushed the Paiutes under its irresistible weight.

Temporarily, he was safe. He walked to the pool to satisfy his own thirst, then sprawled out on his back and rested. Those Paiutes not caught in the defile would rejoin their fellows to report the incident. Depending on whether the rest of the war party had captured the women, the Paiutes would send some warriors after him.

He had time, though, to rest, to replenish his energy before going after the women. Secure in the knowledge the Paiutes were thwarted, he dozed. Now and again he would open his eyes and scan the glen. All was peaceful.

By his reckoning an hour had gone by when he roused himself and stood. He led the Ovaro to the pool and they both drank. Filling the canteen was a moment's work. He noticed one of the ties on the *mochila* had loosened and he tightened the knot before swinging into the saddle and angling up the ancient trail.

A panoramic spectacle spread out before his eyes when he came to the crest. He was a tiny speck in a sea of arid plain. To the north was a small dust cloud, the survivors of his little trap seeking to rejoin their fellows. There were no other dust clouds. Either the women were in Paiute hands or they were too far east for their dust to be seen.

Skye worked his way to the bottom and headed northeast, expecting to come on the trail left by the fleeing foursome and the Paiutes within the hour. When an hour and a half had elapsed and he still hadn't found their tracks, he halted. The only explanation he could think of was that Slade, Howard, and the women had changed the direction of their flight. Since he hadn't come across their sign yet, they couldn't have turned to the south. With the Paiutes to the west, the sole other avenue of escape open to them was to the north, deeper into the heart of Paiute country.

Would Slade and Howard have been so foolish? Rosemary and Lida didn't know any better. They became hopelessly lost once beyond the comfortable confines of a big city, so they would go wherever the men wanted.

Mystified, he pressed due north. Fifteen minutes later he discovered the trail. The tracks of the two shod horses were easy to tell from those of the Paiutes even though the war party had obliterated many of them in passing. Alert for movement or the circling of buzzards, he rode on with the Sharps across his thighs ready for instant use.

The merciless sun beat down on his brow. All the water he had consumed at the pool did little to alleviate the discomfort. Sweat again trickled down his body and coated the pinto. In the distance, so small he could barely see it, was the telltale cloud raised by the survivors from the defile, also heading north.

Skye removed his hat to wipe the inner lining and ran a hand through his damp hair. As he replaced the hat the Ovaro snorted. He saw the reason right away. Sixty yards off lay a dead horse.

Touching his spurs to the pinto, Fargo rode up to the carcass. The cause of death was immediately apparent. There were two arrows jutting from between the animal's ribs. It was an Indian mount, the one Lida had been on.

Plagued by questions he couldn't answer, Skye resumed riding northward. Had Lida been captured? If so, was she still with the war party or had the Paiutes taken her to a village? And what about Rosemary? Was she still with Slade and Howard? From the tracks, it was apparent the war party had almost overtaken the women and the hard cases. The Paiutes had definitely been within bow range. There seemed little hope any of the four were alive.

But Skye Fargo wasn't about to give up. No one had

ever branded him a quitter, and he hadn't acquired the reputation he enjoyed by being a mere flash in the pan. He would stick to the trail until the truth was known, and if the women were dead he would head for the next station and finally pass on the *mochila*. As for Rafe Slade and Pete Howard, they were grown men and their fate was in their own hands. He didn't give a tinker's damn about either one.

The golden sun had climbed high in the azure sky when he came to rough, broken country, crisscrossed by canyons and dotted with jagged plateaus. The tracks led straight into a canyon and he was about to follow them when he heard, faintly, the clatter of hoofs.

A cluster of boulders to his right offered the only concealment, and he promptly rode behind them, swung down, and stood with a hand over the stallion's muzzle to prevent it from nickering. Soon the hoofbeats were close by and he risked a peek around a boulder.

Nine dusty, tired Paiutes had emerged from the canyon. Three of the braves were leading horses bearing bodies of other warriors. They struck off almost due west and were out of sight in minutes.

Had the war party abandoned the chase? Skye wondered. Not very likely. Then what did the departure mean? Were they going for more warriors or fresh horses? And where were the rest? There must be a half-dozen or so unaccounted for. Were they back up the canyon?

Forking the damp saddle, Fargo warily entered the canyon and backtracked the Paiutes. The canyon floor climbed steadily upward in the direction of a barren mountain. He had gone a few hundred yards when a shot echoed from above. Moving into the shadows at the base of the canyon wall, he waited and listened but there was no further gunfire. Who had it been? A Paiute? Slade or Howard?

Hugging the shadows, he rode until a bend obstructed his view. The tracks indicated at least two shod horses had gone around the corner, which meant the two hard cases must be up there somewhere. Sliding to the ground, he stepped forward and peered at what lay beyond.

The canyon ended abruptly not more than two hundred yards distant at the side of the mountain, terminating in a bowl-shaped basin rimmed by boulders that flanked a sheer cliff.

Skye saw no one at first. Then the flick of a tail drew his eyes to three war horses tethered behind a low knoll at the bottom of the slight slope leading up into the basin. Where there were Indian ponies there must be Indians, and a patient scan of possible hiding places turned up two prone braves lying so still they blended perfectly into the landscape. The third must be nearby.

He drew back and mopped his brow, pondering. He figured that Slade and Howard, and possibly one or both of the women, were holed up in the basin. Those three warriors were there to keep the whites pinned down while the rest of the war party went to their village for more braves.

All the Paiutes had to do was wait. Slade and Howard, with their backs to the mountain and no other way out, were hopelessly trapped. Eventually they would run out of what little food and water they had, and then they would have to make a mad dash past the waiting warriors to gain their freedom. By then the other Paiutes would return with reinforcements, and when the two hard cases made their bid they would be cut down in a hail of lead. Or, more likely, the Paiutes would take them alive to indulge in some torture before slaying them.

He must do something, and do it before the rest of the Paiutes came back. Squinting up at the sun, he decided to wait until dark descended. He'd have the element of surprise in his favor and might be able to pull it off.

Fargo gripped the bridle and took the Ovaro to a shady spot where they couldn't be seen from the middle of the canyon. Next he uncorked his canteen and washed out the stallion's nostrils, then let the Ovaro slurp from his hand. It wasn't much, but it would have to do. At last, weary to the bone, he sat down and propped his back against a boulder. There were about two hours to kill until nightfall. Not much time at all, considering they might be the last two hours he would see on this earth.

# 9

The dark gray of twilight shrouded the canyon when Fargo made his move. Sticking to the blackest shadows and utilizing cover as only a man who knew Indian ways could, he advanced toward the basin.

Once, less than half an hour before, another rifle shot had boomed along the canyon walls. Slade or Howard, he had reasoned, perhaps trying to nail a Paiute as the brave changed position. Or maybe the hard cases were so high-strung by now that they were shooting at figments of their own imaginations.

He had taken a risk by waiting for dark. If the Paiute village lay within a few miles of the canyon, the war party would return before he could accomplish his goal. But he doubted the village was anywhere near. From the stories he heard at Salt Lake City and elsewhere, he gathered the Paiutes were based farther west and at this time of year would be somewhere in the vicinity of Pyramid Lake. If so, the war party couldn't possibly get back to the canyon before noon or later tomorrow. He should have the time he needed.

He glided ever nearer, the Arkansas toothpick clutched in his right hand. The Sharps had been left in his saddle scabbard, the Colt rested in its holster. He must dispose of the three Paiutes quickly and silently, and for that there was no better weapon than a knife.

Finding them would be difficult. They weren't about to advertise their presence. And he didn't dare let one of them spot him first or a warning shout would alert the others and ruin his plan.

When he came to the slope below the basin he crouched behind a boulder and listened, tuning his ears to the nocturnal sounds of the canyon. A wind sighed off the mountain, cooling his cheeks. Scouring the slope, he spied a flicker of light reflected off one of the boulders rimming the basin. Someone had a small fire going in there. Lifting his head, he sniffed the air and registered the delicious aroma of boiling coffee.

Hunching low, he slid up behind a stone slab. The coffee scent was stronger. He knew the Paiutes would smell it, too, and wondered if the aroma was doing to their stomachs what it was doing to his. Several times he had to exercise supreme willpower and stop it from growling.

Suddenly, from off on his right, there came the dry rattle of a dislodged pebble as it rolled a few feet.

Fargo instantly crept in the direction of the sound. He would pause every two or three steps and sink onto his knees while probing the night for a brave. On one such occasion he spied a flitting shadow moving from boulder to boulder about a half-dozen feet above him. As near as he could tell, the Paiute was facing up the slope toward the basin. Which was as he'd hoped. Since the three warriors had no idea he was nearby, they would be concentrating on the trapped whites.

He saw the Paiute halt and straighten to study the reflected light. On silent feet he eased up behind the brave and drew back the toothpick. Somehow, perhaps alerted by the sixth sense Indians seemed to develop as a consequence of constantly living in danger, the Paiute sensed something was wrong and started to turn.

Skye Fargo was ready. His left arm looped around the Paiute's windpipe, cutting off any possible sound, as his right arm plunged the knife to the hilt in the warrior's side. Not once, but three times in swift succession. The Paiute, taken completely unawares, could do no more than utter a muffled grunt and flap his arms a time or two. Then the brave died.

Fargo let the man down easy and caught the warrior's bow before it could fall. Holding the smooth wood in his hand, an idea occurred to him and he quickly stooped and removed four arrows from a quiver on the dead Paiute's back. Then he wedged the toothpick under his belt for the time being and set to work again.

The second Paiute was easy to find. He had crawled to within a yard of the boulders at the top, and from where Fargo stood he could see the outline of the brave's face as revealed in the faint reflected light from the campfire. From within the basin the Paiute was no doubt invisible. Not so to anyone on the lower slope.

He notched an arrow, lifted the bow, and slowly drew back the string. A powerful bow, it took all of his strength to bring the string to his chin. He had not shot a bow in more months than he cared to recollect, but he sighted along the shaft as he'd been taught by the Sioux and fixed the barbed point on the center of the Paiute's back. Since he was firing uphill he compensated by elevating the shaft a fraction. Taking a deep breath he held steady, then relaxed his fingers.

The arrow was a blur in the night. Its razor-sharp point struck the Paiute between the shoulder blades and sliced clean through his body to jut out from the middle of his chest. Belatedly, the pain racked his body and he looked down at the bloody tip in amazement. Pivoting, he looked around as if seeking his fellow warriors, then he gripped the slick shaft, staggered a step, and crashed to the ground with a thud.

Fargo dropped low. If the third and last Paiute was anywhere close, he would have heard that noise. It might make him curious and he would come to investigate. Fargo opted to stay put and see what happened. He didn't have long to wait.

A ghostly figure darted from boulder to boulder, moving toward the prone warrior. It paused on seeing the body, then vanished as if swallowed by the very earth.

Now Skye was in trouble. The last brave knew there was an enemy outside of the basin and would be searching for him. A test of nerves would ensue, with the first one who made a noise being the loser. There must be something he could do to prevail, though, and his racing mind hit on a ruse as old as the hills. Old, but effective.

His probing fingers found a small stone. Lifting his right arm, he hurled the stone as far as he could off to the left. Predictably, it made a racket when it landed and bounced a few times.

The ghostly figure reappeared, sweeping toward the spot where the rock had struck.

Fargo already had another arrow nocked. He could have used the Colt, but maybe, just maybe, the Paiute war party might be returning and be near enough to hear it. Not that he believed they were. But he had learned long ago that it paid to err on the side of caution when one's life was on the line.

Halting a few yards uphill, the last of the warriors was silhouetted against a barren patch of soil behind him. The arrow carved a path from his ribs to his armpit, twisting him around from the impact. Gamely, he raised a rifle, but a second shaft nailed him at the base of the throat and he toppled. For a minute he convulsed, blood spurting all over his chest and stomach. The final sight he saw was of a tall man in buckskins who materialized out of nowhere and stood watching him die. He grimaced, trying to hurl a curse at the despised white, but all he could do was spit a crimson spray. Sagging, he died.

Fargo discarded the bow and arrows and picked up the brave's rifle, then ran to the basin rim. Stopping, he called out, "Hello in there! Don't shoot! I'm coming in."

"Who the hell is it?" came Pete Howard's reply.

"It's Skye! He's alive!"

That was Rosemary. Fargo eased between two boulders and she ran up to him and threw her arms around his neck. Crouching to the right was Howard. Slade was on his knees behind a pile of rocks off to the left.

"Oh, God!" Rosemary breathed in his ear. "We thought you were dead!"

Skye eased back and saw tears of relief in her eyes. "Where's Lida?"

Rosemary promptly sobered. "They got her. Shot her horse out from under her and then grabbed her before we could do a thing."

Pete Howard was still under cover. He glanced into the darkness, his brow furrowed. "How did you get in here? There are dozens of Paiutes out there waiting to take our hair."

"Most of the war party rode off earlier," Fargo revealed. "They left three braves to make sure you didn't escape."

"And where are they?" Slade asked, walking over, his rifle cradled in his brawny arms. From the fact he had exposed himself, it was apparent he knew the answer.

Fargo drew a finger across the base of his throat.

"All by your lonesome?" Slade said. "I'm some impressed. Not many men could do that."

Pete Howard stood. "Well, if those devils are gone now is our chance to ride. They'll come back, sure as shootin', and I don't aim to be here when they do."

"You ride if you want," Fargo said. "I'm going after Lida."

"You'll be committing suicide," Howard stated.

"What's she to you?" Slade threw in.

"Nothing," Fargo answered, moving to the fire. He didn't bother getting a cup; he raised the pot to his lips and gulped a few mouthfuls of the steaming hot brew.

"Then why risk your life?" Slade persisted.

Fargo glanced sharply at the tall man. Was Slade genuinely curious or prying for some reason? Western men generally knew better than to delve into the personal affairs of others; such questions sometimes sparked flying lead.

"It's your business," Slade said, his brow furrowed, "but I just don't understand why you would go out and get killed for a woman who doesn't mean a damn thing to you. I know I wouldn't."

"I promised to get her safely to California," Fargo said, and let it go at that. Slade would know what it meant for a man to give his word. Any deeper motivation would be impossible to explain to a man who reputedly possessed no scruples whatsoever.

"What about us?" Rosemary asked.

"Swing south and head for Reese River Station. I'll catch up later if I can."

"I'd rather stay with you."

"Too dangerous."

"Please."

Fargo saw a trace of fear in her eyes, and he knew why. She didn't want to be left alone with Howard and Slade, and he didn't blame her. But taking her with him increased the risk of being spotted by the Paiutes since the closer he got to their village the more of them there would be in the vicinity.

Rafe Slade coughed. "Fargo, if it's all right with you we'll tag along and help you rescue Lida."

Howard gaped. "We'll what?"

"You heard me," Slade growled.

"Have you gone plumb loco?" Howard retorted. "We

86

don't owe these people a thing. It isn't like the woman is kin or even a good friend."

"I'm going."

"Those Paiutes will have your hair."

"I ain't about to argue, Pete," Slade said, and walked toward the horses picketed on the opposite side of the basin at the base of the cliff.

"What the hell has gotten into him?" Howard asked no one in particular. He gestured in exasperation, stared up at the glittering stars, and muttered under his breath. Then he hurried after his companion.

"I figured Slade would just ride off," Rosemary said.

"So did I," Fargo said, and took another swallow of coffee. "This is good. You make it?"

Rosemary nodded. "Slade said we might as well eat and drink a good meal since it might be our last. He said it didn't make a difference if we started a fire because the Paiutes knew where we were anyway."

Fargo took a half step closer to her. "Were Lida and you treated all right?"

She nodded and answered in a hushed voice. "I've been worried about the same thing, but we were so busy trying to stay alive there was no time for anything else." She paused and glanced at the two men by the horses. "I think Slade has taken a shine to Lida."

"Oh?"

"I caught him staring at her once or twice while we were riding and he was real upset when the Paiutes got her. He even started to go back but Howard yelled for him to keep going or he'd be killed."

So that explained it. Fargo downed more coffee. He'd known many a hard man in his time who had been tamed by the flutter of pretty eyes and the blush of lovely cheeks. When a woman started throwing a loop there was always some man ready to step right into the snare and give up the roving life for a home, children, and three squares a day.

"So we can go with you?" Rosemary asked hopefully.

"Yes," Skye said, glad Slade had made the decision. Now he wouldn't have to worry so much about protecting her, and if he had to sneak into a village after Lida he could leave Rosemary in their care.

Slade returned leading two horses. "Here you go,

ma'am," he said, offering the reins of the Indian pony to Rosemary.

"Thank you."

"You're welcome."

Fargo noticed Pete Howard gazing at Slade as if he couldn't quite believe his own eyes, and he had to suppress a laugh. "Whose pot?" he asked, wagging it.

"Mine," Slade said, and emptied out the last of the brew. He stuck the pot into his saddlebags, then mounted.

Fargo went down the slope and retrieved his horse. The others waited while he forked leather, and a moment later they were riding briskly out of the canyon and onto the plain. He was slightly surprised when Rafe Slade rode up beside him.

"Mind if we talk?"

"I didn't think we had anything to talk about."

Slade ignored the remark. "I reckon you've heard as much about me as I have about you."

"A thing or two."

"I'm not as bad as they paint me," Slade said, and sighed. "You know how it is. A man gets into a few fights, maybe has to kill an *hombre* or two just to stay alive, and the next thing he knows he has a reputation as a bad man."

"Why are you telling me this?" Fargo asked, his eyes surveying the plain, tempted to bring up the fact that Slade's reputation consisted of more than a few fights. Slade had killed twelve men or better and had supposedly rustled stock and perhaps robbed a stage or two, although the law didn't have any concrete proof.

"I don't rightly know. I got a feeling, is all." Slade turned toward him. "I've taken a liking to that Lida. She's a fine filly, even if she has worked on the wrong side of the line. She kept looking at me when she was jabbering with Pete. I think she likes me."

Fargo said nothing.

"A man gets tired of wandering after a while," Slade went on. "He starts to think of what it would be like to have his own spread, to prop his feet in front of a fireplace on a cold night and have his woman bring him a hot coffee. Know what I mean?"

"I think so."

"You ever had that urge?"

"Not yet."

"Well, whatever happens, you make certain you get Lida away from those stinking Paiutes. I'm counting on you, mister, and I've never counted on anyone."

"I'll do my best," Fargo pledged, hiding his amazement. Would wonders never cease? He never would have marked Rafe Slade as the marrying kind. The old saying about never judging a book by its cover applied perfectly. He still didn't trust the man, but he was willing to give Slade the benefit of the doubt until Slade proved otherwise.

They had no trouble following the tracks left by the Paiutes, even in the dark. The moon provided enough illumination to reveal the earth churned by the heavy hoofs, a trail that led steadily westward. Over two hours after leaving the basin they found where the band had stopped at a tank, a deep rock hollow that caught and held rain water. Tanks were usually at least partially full during the rainy season, but by late summer most were dry. This one was a third full and they allowed their horses to drink before treating themselves. The water was cool and refreshing.

"I've been thinking," Slade commented. "Three of those bastards rode off with Lida just before we were chased into that canyon. Maybe they didn't take her to the same village this bunch is headed for."

"I'd say they did," Fargo said. "There hasn't been any sign of tracks breaking to the north or south. We'll find her."

"We'd better."

By the time dawn announced its arrival by painting the eastern horizon a shade of bright pink, they were all riding wearily, their shoulders slumped, their mounts plodding mechanically.

Fargo sought a place to hole up for a spell, preferably somewhere with plenty of shade and maybe some water. When a dry wash crossed their path he rode down into it, then reined to the north where a cluster of boulders the size of small houses promised adequate shelter from the scorching heat. The wash went straight through the center of them, and he stopped under an arch formed by two of the boulders that had tilted against one another.

"Are we resting?" Rosemary inquired hopefully, and lifted a tired arm to wipe her palm across her forehead.

"We'll stay here until nightfall," Fargo said.

"What about Lida?" Slade remarked. "I'm for pushing on until we find her."

"In the heat of the day we wouldn't be in any shape to save her," Fargo replied. "If we push it tonight we might find their village by daylight. Then we can slip in and get her out."

Pete Howard made a clucking noise. "You hope it will be that easy but we both know you'll be lucky to slip in and out without having your throat slit. Hell, she could be dead right now for all we know."

"Shut up," Slade said.

"I'm tellin' the truth and you know it," Howard said, refusing to be cowed. "And don't expect me to try and sneak into a Paiute village with you. When the time comes you'll be on your own, pard."

Rafe Slade slid to the ground. "You never did have any grit, you weasel."

"That's no way to talk to me! Not after all the tight scrapes we've been in together."

"And when I need you the most you won't lend a hand."

They began arguing, and Fargo ignored them so he could search among the boulders. Dismounting, he walked along the wash until he discovered a discolored patch of soil under a boulder perched on the right bank. Kneeling, he clawed into the darker earth, his fingers probing for any trace of moisture. Five inches down he touched slightly damp dirt. At seven inches water started to seep up into the hole. He let it fill and then cupped a mouthful to his lips.

The water was muddy and not as cool as he would have liked, but he sipped gratefully, saving the liquid in his canteen for later when he would really need it. Then he relayed the news to the others. They all took turns after watering the horses and staking them in a meager patch of brown grass.

"I'll take first watch," Skye offered. He waited until all three were as comfortable as they could make themselves, then pulled a handful of long grass and returned to the point where the trail crossed the wash. Backing up slowly, he carefully brushed away the hoofprints made when he led his companions to the boulders. Such a trick wouldn't withstand a close scrutiny, so he sprinkled dust over the ground nearest the Paiute tracks as added insurance.

His body swam in sweat when he came back and sat with his spine braced against a boulder. Pete Howard was snoring. Slade and Rosemary were still, their eyes closed.

He didn't know what to make of Slade. Never in a million years would he have expected such a man to become attached to a woman in Lida's line of work. Stranger things had happened, though. And he had learned long ago that matters of the heart were as unpredictable as high country weather. Just as a mountain rider never knew when a storm might sweep down out of nowhere without any warning, so a man could never tell when he might bump into a woman who set his very blood to storming with uncontrollable desire.

And maybe, just maybe, Rafe Slade had grown tired of the outlaw trail. When some men were young in years and as green as fresh alfalfa, they were attracted to a way of life that promised excitement and lots of money and all the wild women they could rope in. But a few years of robbing and running served to convince all but the really dumb ones that outlaws were commonly called polecats for a very simple reason: the way of life stunk. A man got tired of always looking over his shoulder, of never knowing if the next stranger he met might be a lawman out for his hide. Perhaps Slade had come to the same conclusion.

Shortly before noon Skye awakened Slade and Howard. Rosemary, he let sleep. She badly needed the rest since she was exhausted from their ordeal and the end was nowhere in sight. Placing his ground sheet and blankets near her, he tugged off his boots, eased onto his back, and tried to fall asleep.

His mind refused to cooperate. Several times he glanced at his saddle and the *mochila*, lying next to his feet. He couldn't wait to dispose of the Express mail. If not for that Pony Express rider, he would have been well away from the territory by now, safe in California.

At last he slipped into a fitful slumber, and the time

must have passed swiftly because the next time he opened his eyes the shadows were long, the sun setting. He opened them because he had felt pressure on his lips, and there, looming above him with one hand on his mouth and the other holding a six-shooter, was Rafe Slade.

# 10

"The mangy Paiutes," Slade whispered, and motioned with his head as he removed his hand.

Sitting up, Fargo could see back down the wash. He glimpsed a large war party crossing it, enveloped in their own dust, a couple of dozen yards south of where he had erased their tracks. It must be the band from the canyon returning with extra braves. How many, he couldn't tell, although he guessed well over fifty. Those Paiutes were in for a nasty surprise when they reached the basin, and they wouldn't like it one bit. The first thing they would do was scour the countryside. "We have to get the hell out of here," he said softly.

Slade nodded. "Pete is saddling our horses. I'll watch while you saddle yours."

Rosemary, Skye noticed, was still sleeping like the proverbial baby, her breasts rising and falling rhythmically. He saw the last of the war party pass from sight, then grabbed his boots and upended them to make sure a wandering scorpion or snake hadn't moved in while he slept. After pulling the boots on he stood and stamped his feet a few times until they were comfortable.

Adjusting his hat, Fargo stepped to his saddle, hoisted it and the *mochila*, and hurried to the pinto. Howard was just finishing with Slade's horse, having already saddled his.

"Are the damn Paiutes gone?"

"For now. But they'll be back," Fargo said, depositing his load.

"I've done some stupid things in my time, but this beats all," Howard grumbled. "We should be hightailing it to Californy instead of riding deeper into Piaute country. No woman is worth losing your hair over."

"Ride off if you want," Fargo said. He checked the

saddle blanket to see if it was free of burrs and dirt, then flipped it onto the Ovaro.

"All alone?" Howard responded, and snorted. "How long do you reckon I'd last? A lone rider wouldn't stand a chance, not unless he's Injun savvy and desert savvy like you. No thank you, Mr. Trailsman. I'll go where Slade goes."

Fargo lifted his saddle. "Once Lida is safe we'll make for the border. In two days you could be drinking wine in California."

"In two days we could all be pincushions."

The hard case drifted off, leading the two horses. Fargo soon trailed after him, the pinto and Rosemary's mount in tow. Rosemary was awake. All four animals were permitted to drink before the four of them climbed aboard.

"You shouldn't have let me sleep so long," she said. "I'm perfectly capable of keeping watch."

"You may yet get to," Fargo replied, and rode south along the wash bed until he reached the crossing point. Off to the east a misty plume marked the location of the war party. With a cluck and a jab of his spurs he headed westward once again.

If luck was with them, they would not need to travel all the way to Pyramid Lake to find Lida. The Paiutes had more than one village, and it was possible she had been taken to a closer encampment. Either way, there would be more prowling bands about, both mounted and on foot. He must stay alert every second or suffer the consequences.

When the moon rose he let himself relax a bit. By now the majority of Paiutes were settled down for the night, either in their lodges or around a campfire out on the plain. By the pale moonlight he tracked the war party, continuing on until past midnight.

"Our horses could use a break," Rosemary commented.

Fargo had been thinking the same thing. They were in a dry valley between two hillocks approximately five hundred yards apart. "We'll take a half hour to rest," he proposed, and pointed at the western hillock. "Rosemary and I will go up there. Slade, you and Howard take the eastern hill. If you see anything, come running."

"Why do we have to split up?" Pete Howard asked testily. "It would be smarter to stay together."

"No, it wouldn't," Slade said. "This way no one can get at us from either side. Fargo's idea is fine." He turned to retrace his steps to the eastern hillock.

Glaring spitefully, Howard spun his horse and cantered away.

"That man doesn't like you," Rosemary said.

"Howard doesn't like anyone but himself," Fargo responded, moving toward their resting place. A refreshingly cool breeze fanned his face as he came to the top and climbed down.

"Care to give a girl a hand?"

Fargo stepped over, reached up to take her under the arms, and slowly lowered her to the bare ground. She pressed against him, deliberately mashing her breasts against his chest, and entwined her fingers in his hair. "What do you think you're doing?" he demanded.

"I haven't had you to myself since we left that last station," Rosemary said, grinning, and pecked him on the chin.

"Are you crazy? We're in the middle of a Paiute uprising."

"That didn't stop you at the station." She nibbled on his neck, then licked his earlobe.

"We were indoors," Fargo said, making a halfhearted effort to push her away. Despite himself, his manhood was surging to attention and he felt a familiar fire in his veins. "Here we're out in the open, for crying out loud."

Rosemary giggled. "No one can see us. And you can keep a lookout while I indulge myself."

"You *are* crazy. Now of all times?"

"It's more exciting this way," Rosemary said, and lathered his neck with her tongue. "Please. I need it."

His skin tingling, Fargo glanced at the horses. Should anyone approach, the animals would instantly let him know. Still, he felt compelled to try one more time. "If you think I'm taking off my clothes out here, you're mistaken," he said huskily.

"Who said anything about taking off our clothes?"

That did it. After all he had been through, after all the fighting and the long hours spent in the saddle coupled with the sustained strain of constantly being on his guard, Fargo liked the idea of a little much-deserved re-laxation. He knew it was insane, knew it might qualify as downright dumb, but he couldn't help himself. The soft feel of her breasts and the swell of her pubic mound as it touched his groin aroused all of his latent desire and he let his hands rove over her clothes.

"I want you," Rosemary whispered. "I may never get to make love again."

Was that it? Skye wondered in the back of his mind. Did she expect to be slain or captured by the Paiutes so she wanted to know the thrill of passionate lovemaking one more time? Whatever her motivation, he fully in-tended to oblige her. Their burning lips touched and locked, their tongues became as one. Her hot breath mingled with his, her hands ran up and down his back.

His own hands were busy. From her breasts he lowered them to her buttocks and pushed inward on her poste-rior, grinding her mound and thighs into his loins even harder than before. She quivered and played with his hair, breathing heavily into his ear.

Both the Ovaro and the Indian pony were idly munch-ing snippets of grass. Neither exhibited any telltale alarm or nervousness. The westerly breeze bore no disturbing scents.

Keeping an eye cocked toward the animals, Fargo slid a hand between Rosemary's legs, the folds of her dress clinging to his fingers. Even through the fabric he felt the furnace of her slit, and he rubbed his forefinger back and forth to let the friction increase her pleasure and need. Her willowy legs clamped on his hand as she cooed softly.

Perhaps it was the insanity of the moment, or the ex-citement of lovemaking under such hazardous conditions, but they both become fully aroused in no time and their bodies were flush from head to toe.

Fargo kept rubbing her nether lips, feeling the heat intensify and the material become damp with her juices. At length, when she was squirming uncontrollably, he hoisted her hem until he could slip his hand under her dress, part her undergarments, and plunge two fingers into her womanhood.

Rosemary arched her spine and gasped. "Oh, God!" she whispered. "That feels so *good*."

"How about this?" Fargo responded as he pumped his fingers in and out. She panted and drenched his hand, her legs trembling like wild.

Suddenly Fargo felt her hands on his pants, and then she slid them to his belt buckle and frantically jerked on it, trying to free his organ. "Allow me," he said, and drew back a few inches to accomplish the task. As his manhood sprang loose her fingers closed on the shaft.

"Lord, you're huge!"

He could say nothing. It took all of his self-control to keep from expending prematurely as her deft hands stroked him up and down. His whole body seemed to swell with lustful abandon. He bent his neck and locked his lips on hers, his tongue probing far back into her mouth.

Expelling a long breath through her nose, Rosemary ground the entire length of her body into him as if trying to climb inside his skin. Her inner thighs were slick with moisture from her bubbling inner core.

Fargo reached a hand behind her and gripped her fanny securely, then hoisted her upward. She knew what he wanted done and obligingly widened her legs, curling them around his hips. The tip of his pole brushed her slit and they both trembled.

"Oh, yes!" she sighed. "Do me, lover!"

He wedged two fingers into her nether lips, then eased his disgorged shaft in their wake, sliding all the way in until his pubic hairs mingled with hers. Her sheath closed around him in a perfect fit and he held still, savoring the moment.

"God, you're terrific!"

Skye put both hands on her buttocks and started moving her up and down. She helped by using her thighs as if riding a horse, falling into a natural erotic rhythm, all the while planting fiery kisses on his face and neck. He closed his eyes for a few seconds, lost in ecstasy, then remembered where he was and the predicament they were in and opened them again to stare at the Ovaro. Only with a supreme effort could he pay any attention to the stallion. His body had a mind of its own and wanted to indulge in uncontrolled coupling. But he knew the risk they were running. He knew he must stay alert.

Damn it all.

The minutes passed ever so slowly. They kissed, fondled one another, and remained joined below their waists.

Fargo paced himself, seeking to delay the moment of truth for as long as he could. She felt so good, though, that ultimately he couldn't prevent the inevitable. Rosemary brought the climax on by suddenly arching her back, panting crazily, and ramming herself onto him as if striving to be impaled from slit to throat.

"Oh, God! I'm coming, handsome! I'm coming!"

On cue his organ throbbed as if about to explode, and then did. He let himself go, slamming into her, his pole spurting mightily. Every pore in his body seemed to tingle with sheer delight.

Skye saw the Ovaro abruptly lift its head and gaze eastward, its ears pricked, and since he was facing due west he couldn't tell what the pinto had seen. But it couldn't be Indians, he told himself, because Slade and Howard were watching to the east and they would have warned him with a shout or a shot if the Paiutes had appeared.

Still, he didn't like having his back exposed and vulnerable. He rushed now, pounding into her womanhood until he was spent. Then, regretfully, he pulled out of her, his right hand dropping to the Colt as he spun on his boot heels and peered into the night.

"Ohhhhhhh," Rosemary said, sagging against his side, her eyes shut, oblivious to everything except her sexual joy.

Fargo saw nothing at first. He scanned right and left, thinking the Ovaro might have been spooked by a passing animal, a coyote or even a rabbit. Then he spied the black bulk silhouetted against the backdrop of the starry firmament. It was a horse and rider, perhaps forty feet out. Instantly he cocked the big revolver.

The distinct click carried far in the clear air.

"Hold on there, Fargo! It's me! Pete Howard."

"Come on in," Skye said, wondering how long the man had been out there. Had Howard been watching him and Rosemary the whole time? The thought made his skin crawl.

At the hard case's hail Rosemary had straightened and smoothed her dress, trying to compose herself. She brushed her hair into place and took several deep breaths to stabilize her breathing. The look she shot at Skye showed that she was thinking along the same lines as he was.

"Slade sent me over," Howard said as he approached, a peculiar grin curling his thin lips. He rubbed a hand on the stubble covering his chin and gazed brazenly at Rosemary.

"If you have something to say, say it," Fargo snapped.

"Sure enough, Mr. Trailsman," Howard replied sarcastically. "Rafe said to tell you he thinks we've got Paiutes on our tail. It's hard to see far, even with our field glasses, but he thought he spotted riders coming over a ridge about a mile and a half back."

"Then we press on now," Fargo said. "Go get Rafe."

"Rafe, is it?" Howard said, and chuckled. "On my way." He turned his horse and trotted off.

"I don't trust that man," Rosemary commented.

"That makes two of us," Fargo told her. "Get mounted. We'll have to ride like hell if we want to save Lida. We have to get to the Paiute village well ahead of any pursuit."

They were in the saddle when Slade and Howard galloped up, and without a word the four of them rode westward. Slade took the lead and maintained a steady, fast pace for the next hour and a half. Coming over a rise, they reined up in surprise at discovering a narrow but verdant valley situated in the middle of the vast arid expanse they had been crossing. They all smelled the dank scent of water and saw grass growing in profusion. Approximately a quarter of a mile distant stretched a line of trees.

"Never knew this was here," Pete Howard said.

"Make a dandy spot to have a village," Slade remarked.

"Yep," Fargo said, scouring the valley, and then twisted to the north as the wind carried to his ears the unmistakable sound of a barking dog.

"Is that what I think it is?" Howard asked.

"A dog," Slade said, nodding in satisfaction. He drew his six-shooter and began checking the cartridges in the cylinder.

"What's a dog doing way out here?" Rosemary inquired.

"Most tribes own dogs," Fargo explained. "Use them

to keep watch at night and eat them when game is scarce."

"I could never eat one, no matter how hungry I was," Rosemary said, grimacing. "How revolting."

"If you're hungry enough you'll eat anything," Fargo assured her.

"Ain't that the truth," Rafe Slade agreed, and laughed bitterly. "Once, ma'am, I had to eat a rattler raw. It almost made me sick, but at the time it was either eat that sidewinder or starve to death and I didn't cotton to dying right then."

Fargo rode out. He didn't bother to shuck the Sharps. When and if the time came for gunplay, the enemy would probably be up close where a revolver was the handier weapon. The dog had ceased making noise but he had the general direction fixed in his mind and forged ahead until they were in a grove of willows and other trees. Reining up, he slid to the ground and handed his reins to Rosemary. "Hold on to these while I scout up ahead."

"I'm going with you," Slade said, climbing down.

"You can count me out," Howard stated. "I'll stay right here where it's safe."

"Take care of Rosemary," Slade told him.

"You can bet I will."

Something about Howard's tone gave Skye pause. He didn't like leaving Rosemary alone with the weasel, but he discounted the notion that Howard would try anything when they were this close to a Paiute village. One scream would rouse every warrior. Besides which, Pete Howard was essentially a coward, a back-shooter who had long relied on Rafe Slade to get them out of any serious trouble. Howard wasn't about to bother Rosemary if it meant being forced to flee, alone, across miles and miles of countryside crawling with war parties.

"Don't let my horse wander off," Slade said to his partner. "I may need it in a hurry."

"I'll watch it," Howard promised.

Fargo smiled at Rosemary, then melted into the trees. He had to move as quietly as a ghost since Indian dogs were notoriously sharp of hearing. Another concern was the wind. At the moment it was blowing from the northwest to the southeast, carrying their scent away from the village. Should it reverse direction, though, as the fickle winds in those parts were prone to do, their scent would be detected by the dogs and there would be hell to pay.

Rafe Slade was off to the right a dozen yards, his revolver out and cocked.

Sooner than expected Skye came on the Paiute camp and promptly dropped into a crouch. The trees ended twenty feet ahead. Beyond were about thirty typical Paiute dwellings. Because the tribe was nomadic and seldom spent more than a month in the same spot, the Paiutes built open-topped conical structures out of reeds and brush draped over a pole frame. A wide opening, invariably facing to the south or the southeast, afforded entry.

From where Fargo crouched he could see into the majority of the dwellings. Paiutes occupied every one, all sound asleep. Here and there the embers of small fires glowed red. Scattered around the encampment, slumbering restlessly as was their habit, were six or seven dogs. Nowhere was there any sign of Lida.

A twig crunched softly and Slade was at Skye's side. "One of us has to go in there," he whispered.

"I know," Fargo said, wishing it were otherwise. But the only way to find Lida was by checking the interior of each structure, and they didn't have much time in which to accomplish their task. The war party was hard on their trail and might arrive within the hour. A thought occurred to him and he stared at the dwellings again.

"I'll go," Slade volunteered. "Cover my ass if the warriors wake up."

"There might not be many braves there," Fargo said.

"Why not?" Slade responded, and then the obvious hit him and he grinned. "That's right! Almost all the bucks must be with the war party." He nodded at the camp. "Most of them are probably women and kids."

"Most, but not all. The Paiutes wouldn't leave their village undefended."

"I'm not scared of a few scrawny Injuns."

"Paiute women can shoot bows and guns if pressed, and there will be older boys in camp who are every bit as dangerous as their fathers. We can't take them lightly."

Slade snorted and began to move away.

"No," Fargo whispered, grabbing the man's arm. "I'm going in. You're the one who will cover me."

"Why you?" Slade replied.

"I'm better at this sort of thing than you are," Fargo said bluntly. "If Lida is here, I'll find her. Don't worry."

The hard case pondered for a bit, then reluctantly nodded. "All right. But if those redskins give you any trouble, I'm coming in."

Skye crept forward, every nerve on a razor's edge. He took several short, silent steps, then paused for five seconds to look and listen, then repeated the tactic until he was within a few yards of the nearest dwelling and could hear someone snoring lightly. None of the dogs had stirred, and they were his greatest concern.

Inside the first dwelling was a woman and two boys about ten years of age. In the second was another woman with a girl. In the third a warrior and his family of five. And so it went as Skye moved from structure to structure without finding a trace of Lida.

He had checked fourteen of the conical structures and was walking quietly toward the next one when from out of a dwelling further on there shuffled a Paiute boy not more than five years old who turned and gazed directly at him.

# 11

Fargo tensed, bracing for the uproar that would ensue when the child yelled. To his astonishment, there was no outcry. Instead, the boy gazed calmly at him and then rubbed his tired eyes as if he couldn't believe what he was seeing. Pivoting, the child went back into the dwelling.

With not a moment to lose Fargo darted behind the closest structure and sank to his knees. He heard low voices, that of the boy and a woman, and then a few muffled footsteps as the mother stepped outside to look for herself. A few moments later there was another exchange of words, then quiet reigned.

He let his breath out slowly and stood warily. No one was around. Evidently the mother had decided the child had imagined the whole incident. Holding the Colt level, he skirted the back of the dwelling and finally discovered his first clue.

Fifteen feet off was yet another structure. In front of this one, firmly imbedded in the earth, was a large stake. A heavy rope led from the stake into the dwelling.

Fargo leaned down and drew his toothpick. On cat's feet he inched up to the opening and peeked within. It took a few seconds for his eyes to adjust to the inky confines, but finally he distinguished the outline of a sleeping warrior and one other person.

Lida.

Easing to his knees, he applied the toothpick to the rope, slicing slowly, methodically parting strand after strand until the rope was completely severed. Then, exercising infinite care, he moved into the shelter until he was next to Lida. Placing the heel of his left palm on her shin, he gently shook her leg. She stirred but didn't awaken. Again he shook her leg, and this time she mumbled and tossed but still didn't open her eyes.

The woman slept like a log.

Skye shook harder, hoping she would have the good sense not to give him away when she saw him. Lida mumbled some more and her eyes fluttered a few times before finally snapping wide open. He lifted a finger to his lips to warn her to be quiet, only he was too late.

"Skye!" Lida practically screamed, sitting up. "Thank God you've come!"

The Paiute warrior was instantly on his feet, a long knife clutched in his hand, the blade glinting dully in the darkness.

Fargo shot him, a single slug that ripped into the brave's chest and sent the Paiute staggering backward into the rear wall where he collapsed. Outside dogs barked and shouts erupted all over the village. "Are you sure you couldn't have yelled a little louder?" he snapped at Lida, and dashed out.

Shadows flitted in the night. The Paiutes were milling about in confusion, most of them sluggish from having been startled out of a heavy sleep and uncertain of exactly where the shot came from.

Fargo motioned for Lida to get her fanny out of the shelter. So far they were lucky. None of the Paiutes had bothered to get a fire going or to light a torch and in the dark none of the Indians had yet seen him clearly, but that would undoubtedly change at any moment.

Having realized her blunder, Lida sheepishly joined him. The rope dangled from around her neck. "Sorry," she said softly. "I didn't think."

Skye didn't waste time speaking. He also didn't want her tripping over the rope as they fled so he holstered the Colt and used both hands and the toothpick to free her, keenly aware he was wasting precious seconds better spent in headlong flight. As the rope fell there was a sharp cry to his rear and the patter of rushing feet.

He pivoted, drawing the Colt in a blur, his thumb pulling the hammer back even before the revolver was level. Not eight feet away a brave charged with an upraised tomahawk. He terminated the charge with a slug to the brain, then wedged the knife under his belt, grasped Lida's wrist, and raced for the trees.

Now some of the Paiutes realized what was happening and their yells directed others to the scene. They swarmed from all directions, eager to cut off the escaping whites.

Fargo spied a youth of seventeen or so rushing him while notching an arrow to a bow. A snap shot toppled the young Paiute in his tracks.

"Oh, God!" Lida wailed, the whites of her eyes showing bright in the gloom.

He nearly wrenched her off her feet when he broke into an all-out run, glancing every which way at the converging Paiutes. He was hopelessly outnumbered and there were only three unused cartridges in his six-shooter.

A burly brave sprang from behind a dwelling and lunged, a knife in his right hand.

Fargo saw the man appear, saw the blade sweeping at his chest, and desperately tried to avoid the point by letting go of Lida and hurling himself to the side. A stinging pang lanced his left arm and he retaliated by firing at nearly point-blank range into the warrior's face.

Screeching and clutching at his head, the Paiute went down.

Skye had only two shots left. Again he grabbed Lida and sprinted for the woods. Many of the Indians, mainly women and younger children, had stopped or were seeking cover, fearful of his pistol. But there were still plenty trying to overtake him. He couldn't hope to stop them all.

When a mere ten feet from the last of the conical structures he spotted two lean youths attacking from the west. Both held bows, and the instant his eyes alighted on them one of the pair loosed his shaft. Skye whipped his head back with barely a hair to spare as the arrow cleaved the very air his head had just occupied, its feathers brushing the tip of his nose in passing. He lifted the Colt and squeezed off his next-to-last round.

The young Paiute who hadn't fired dropped.

Fargo never slowed. Lida, though, was dragging her feet, perhaps from fatigue, perhaps because she was scared to death. Regardless, he yanked on her arm and was within a few feet of the trees and wondering what the hell had happened to Slade when two warriors dashed toward him, one from either side, both carrying tomahawks. He slowed and took a hasty bead on the nearest, but he wasn't quite fast enough.

Rafe Slade burst from cover with his revolver blazing, shooting to the left and the right so quickly the shots nearly sounded as one. The two tomahawk wielders pitched to the ground. "Run!" Rafe bellowed. "Get her out of here! I'll cover you!" He proceeded to do just that by moving between Fargo and the village and shooting yet another Paiute who intended to thwart their flight.

Skye ran into the woods and stopped, his fingers flying as he reloaded. "We're clear!" he yelled. "Let's go!"

Nodding, Slade backpedaled, his gun booming twice, slaying another young brave. "Keep going!" he urged, glancing over his shoulder. "Take her to the horses!"

About to comply, Fargo glimpsed a scarecrow figure spring out of the nearest dwelling and saw it was an elderly Paiute woman. She held a lance. "Look out!" he warned, trying to bring the Colt to bear.

Slade faced front, recognized the danger, and got off a shot at the very instant the woman threw the lance. With only six feet between them, he was unable to dodge the streaking weapon. It caught him high on the left thigh and sliced clean through the leg. He buckled, falling as the old woman did, landing on his right knee.

"Rafe!" Lida shrieked.

"Don't move!" Fargo roared at her, and darted to Slade's side. The hard case was striving to pull the lance out, his hands coated with his blood. "Lean on me," Fargo directed, and looped an arm around Slade's shoulders to help him stand.

Few Paiutes were in evidence. A boy not much older than ten popped out of nowhere and let fly with a knife, but in his eagerness and inexperience he missed by a yard and immediately vanished.

Fargo retreated into the relative shelter of the woods, then stopped. He could tell Rafe Slade was in tremendous agony and had already lost a great amount of blood. Taking the lance out would cause the wound to bleed even worse, yet it couldn't be helped. Slade couldn't very well flee otherwise. "That has to come out," he said.

"Do it," Slade responded through clenched teeth, on

his knees. He fumbled at his pistol, starting to replace the spent shells. "I'll cover you."

A glance showed Skye the Paiutes had temporarily withdrawn. Kneeling, he clamped both hands on the sturdy shaft, his palms becoming slick with blood. "All set?"

"Ready."

There was only one way to take a lance out. Doing so slowly caused too much pain and sometimes made the wounded party pass out. Twisting the shaft likewise added to the anguish. The best method was a short, sharp jerk, and Fargo bunched his shoulder muscles in preparation.

"An Indian!" Lida suddenly shouted, pointing.

Slade's gun blasted twice, then he looked down at Skye. "Don't dawdle on my account."

In a smooth, powerful motion, his muscles rippling, Fargo pulled with all of his might. The lance slipped out as if greased and more blood sprayed from the neat hole, drenching Slade's pants and splattering Fargo's cheeks and chin. He tossed the lance aside and stood, wiping a sleeve across his face.

"What now?" Lida asked.

"We get the hell out of here," Fargo answered, helping Slade to stand. Slade's bleeding leg almost buckled but the hard case grunted and stayed upright. "There's nothing I can do about your wound until we put this village far behind," he mentioned.

"I know. Let's skedaddle."

They hurried away, Skye making for the spot where Rosemary and Howard waited with the horses. Pete Howard, true to his cowardly word, had failed to come to their aid.

"I don't see any Paiutes after us," Lida commented.

"Most of the warriors are gone," Fargo said. "I imagine we killed those who had stayed behind, and the women and children aren't about to tackle two men armed with guns."

"Oh. Come to think of it, I didn't see very many men in their camp," Lida said.

Slade grew weaker the farther they went. Fargo was hard-pressed to hold the man up and still keep an eye on their back trail. His hunch about the Paiute men had proven correct, but there might be a woman brave enough to sneak up on them and put an arrow in their backs.

Lida moved in on the other side of Slade to lend a hand, pressing her body flush with his and slipping her arm under his armpit. "Where's Rosemary?" she asked.

"Just up ahead," Fargo revealed. He gazed through the trees, eager to spy their horses, but a minute went by without sign of them. In the middle of a small clearing he halted and angrily looked down at the ground. "Son of a bitch!" he growled.

"What's wrong?" Lida inquired.

"This is it."

"This is what?"

"Where Rosemary and Howard were supposed to be waiting for us."

Lida recoiled in shock. "Are you certain?"

"Of course," Skye responded, his fury mounting. Removing his hold on Slade, he squatted and placed his left hand flat on the ground. By running his fingers back and forth he had no difficulty finding the distinctly imprinted fresh horse tracks. "They rode off while Slade and I were in the village."

"Why would they do that?" Lida wanted to know.

"Your guess is as good as mine," Fargo said, although he had an idea that caused his anger to rise to new heights.

Rafe Slade had been sagging against Lida, his head slumped and nearly touching his chest. Grunting from the effort, he straightened and scanned the grove. "Damn that Pete all to hell! When I get my hands on him I'm fixing to end our partnership."

"I'm not sure I understand," Lida said. "What's going on?"

"We must keep going," Fargo declared. He didn't want her to have to worry about Rosemary on top of all their other problems, such as how to elude the Paiutes in the village and the war party that would shortly arrive and how to keep Slade alive long enough to reach California and a doctor.

He took hold of Slade once more and hurried them to the southwest. At the edge of the grove he paused to scrutinize the lay of the land. In front of them lay the long tract of lush grass. To their right was the line of trees he had noted on first entering the valley, and where there were trees in a row like that there was usually a stream, creek, or river. "That way," he directed, and guided Slade toward them.

"I'm scared," Lida said timidly. "If the Paiutes catch me again, I know they'll kill me. The only reason they left me alive the first time was because that warrior you shot took a fancy to me."

Slade's head bobbed. "Don't worry, ma'am. We won't let them redskins get you."

"I feel safer with you to protect me," Lida said, smiling up into his face.

Cupid strikes again! Fargo reflected, and nearly laughed out loud. So Lida had indeed taken a shine to Slade. The workings of the human heart never ceased to amaze him. Here they were in hostile Indian country, with roving bands of bloodthirsty Paiutes slaying any and all whites, without their horses and meager supplies, with only two guns at their disposal, and a limited amount of ammunition, with one of them seriously wounded, and yet Slade and Lida were apparently falling in love. It was enough to make a man suspect that if there really and truly was a God, then He possessed one hell of a sense of humor.

The soft gurgling of gently flowing water led them right to a ribbon of a stream meandering southward along the valley floor. Fargo took shelter in the thick undergrowth on the east bank and carefully deposited Rafe Slade at the base of a tree where the man could prop his back on the trunk. Then he grabbed Slade's hat and went to the stream for water.

Other than a faint breeze, all was still. From the distant village came shouts and there were pinpoints of light flickering in the grove.

Fargo guessed the Paiutes were using torches to search in every thicket and behind every willow near their village. If there were no warriors left alive, the women and older boys would soon give up and wait until dawn. Of course, by then the war party might return and a general sweep of the valley would be conducted. He must locate a better hiding place to secrete Slade and Lida, then try to lead the Paiutes on a wild goose chase.

He filled the hat and hastened back. Slade was barely conscious. Lida sat beside him, affectionately stroking his perspiring brow.

"The poor man," she commented. "He nearly gave his life for me."

Fargo wanted to remind her that he had done the same thing, but he held his peace. Women in love tended to regard their lovers through biased eyes. "Get as much of this into him as you can before it leaks out," he instructed her, and put the hat in her hands. "Then wash the wound."

Pivoting, he stealthily scouted south along the stream. Nowhere did he see a likely spot to hide. When he had gone over two hundred yards he heard the crackling of brush off to the left and flattened, drawing the Colt. A large shape materialized, a riderless horse of all things, coming toward him. Suspecting a trick, he warily rose to his knees. It was then he recognized the telltale mixed light and dark markings of a pinto and grinned.

It was the Ovaro.

The big stallion, its reins dragging, came right over. Skye stroked its neck and spoke softly while trying to figure out how his horse came to be where it was. The best conclusion he could reach was that somehow the Ovaro had tugged loose from Howard and gotten away, then instinctively retraced its steps to find its master. Some horses were like bloodhounds in that respect.

He twirled the Colt into his holster, grasped the reins, and swung up. Continuing south, in five minutes he found where the stream flowed out of the valley through a gap between a pair of bare hills. Erosion had formed steep walls on both sides of the gap, and with his mental fingers crossed he rode into the middle of the ankle-deep water. Near total blackness engulfed him. The Ovaro acted skittish until he rubbed between its ears.

By alternately leaning right and left, Skye could just barely make out the earthen walls. He repeatedly reached out to touch the sides. Toward the center of the gap he found the site he wanted. He saw an area that stood out darker than all the rest and climbed down to investigate. A careful inspection disclosed a small cave hollowed out of the hill by rushing water during periodic flash floods in the spring. Not more than seven feet from front to back, it was a good yard above the current water level. Invisible from the end of the gap, a Paiute would have to be right on it before he knew it was there even in broad daylight.

He lost no time in returning to Slade and Lida. She had Rafe's head nestled in her lap.

"I thought you must be an Indian. Where did you find your horse?"

"Not far off," Fargo replied, sliding down. "How is he holding up?"

"He's weak as a kitten and feels like he's burning up."

"I've found a spot where you should be safe until I can rustle up some mounts," Fargo revealed. "Help me get him onto mine."

It took some doing. Rafe Slade was a big, heavy man. But together they hoisted him into the saddle and held him there. Fargo gripped the bridle and navigated the pinto back to the gap.

"You expect us to stay in *there*?" Lida asked, aghast at the stygian defile.

"It's the safest spot we're likely to find. And there's plenty of water."

She voiced no further objections and assisted in placing Slade on his back in the cave. As Skye turned to leave she clutched his arm. "Please don't be gone long. I—I don't like being hemmed in like this. If they do find us we'll have nowhere to go."

"I'll hurry," Fargo pledged, stepping into the stirrups. "If the Paiutes do find you, you should be able to hold them off for a while with Slade's pistol. They can't approach the cave without being seen and they can't shoot into the cave from above because the walls are too steep. Keep your eyes peeled and you'll be fine." In the dark he could barely see her face, but he could sense her fear. Here was a woman accustomed to city life, to the comfortable parlors and the polite if lewd society of other fallen doves and the men willing to pay for an hour or so of intimate companionship. The only violence she ever saw was when a drunk became too rowdy or a customer became dissatisfied. And here she was swept up in an Indian uprising, fighting for her life against overwhelming odds in a wild, remote territory as far removed from the refined societies of Denver and San Francisco as the earth was from the moon. He could understand how she must be feeling.

He handed over most of his jerky, then bent and gave her shoulder a reassuring squeeze. "I'll be back soon. I promise." With that he rode back into the valley and stopped to listen. The Paiutes had ceased their search in the grove near the village. Other than the sigh of the breeze and the whispering stream the night was deceptively tranquil.

Which way should he go? He must rescue Rosemary quickly, and to do that he must think like Pete Howard. He doubted the bastard had taken her eastward for the simple reason the war party was approaching from that direction. He also doubted Howard had found the gap through the hills that would have taken them due west since Howard would have been in a hurry to get away before Slade or himself returned from the village, which was to the north. By the process of elimination this left due south.

He turned the pinto and made for the southern end of the valley, listening to the long grass brush against the pinto's legs. Somewhere an owl hooted and out on the plain a coyote serenaded the night. At the base of a hill he glanced over his shoulder and it was then he saw the war party.

The braves were just entering the valley from the east and were too far off to tell how many comprised the band. Soon they would arrive at their village and be informed of the escape. Within fifteen minutes they would be scouring every nook and cranny within miles of their stronghold.

Skye yanked out the Sharps. If he could draw the war party off it would delay the search that much longer. He fed in a cartridge, adjusted the rear sight to allow for the range and the fact the Paiutes were a hundred feet or so lower than he was, and sighted on the very center of the close-knit braves. They had altered course for the grove when he held his breath to steady the Sharp's short barrel, and fired.

Like booming thunder the shot crashed across the valley. A Paiute fell and the rest were thrown into confusion. So were their horses.

Fargo sent a second slug into the packed mass before

they could think to separate and seek cover. This time some of the Paiutes spotted the muzzle flash and instantly a half-dozen broke from the pack and streaked toward him. He slid the rifle into its scabbard, applied his spurs to the Ovaro, and went up and over the hill with the wind whipping his hair.

Below stretched countless miles of dry prairie. There was yucca and low brush plants, mesquite and sage. Thankfully the Ovaro was rested enough to gallop over a mile in a zigzag pattern without a hint of fatigue.

Fargo slowed to study his back trail. Apparently he had lost the Paiutes. Now he could concentrate on finding that damned Howard and Rosemary. As he faced front a faint sound from off in the benighted distance sparked apprehension that he might be too late.

It was a shot.

# 12

The rustic miner's cabin lay to the west of a high stone ridge near a spring. A few scrawny trees afforded scant shade from the burning sun. Tied to one of those trees was Pete Howard's horse and the Indian pony Rosemary had been riding.

Fargo watched and waited for over an hour in the hope Howard would emerge from the cabin and give him a clear shot. But no one appeared, forcing him to take action. He had been up all night and weariness threatened to impair his thinking and dull his reflexes. He must move now, while he was still alert.

The sun had been up for less than two hours. Already the rocks were like an oven to the touch and threw off waves of heat. He worked his way along the top of the ridge and found where Howard had descended. A few boulders screened him from the cabin until he was near the bottom. There he reconnoitered and debated his next move.

No brush grew within thirty yards of the building. Anyone trying to get close would be easy pickings. And there was always the risk of Howard's horse neighing if it saw someone coming.

The safest recourse was to wait until nightfall, but Fargo didn't dare. If Rosemary was still alive, she wouldn't be for long. He snaked onto his belly, holding the Sharps in front of his body, and began crawling toward the northwest corner of the cabin. The front and only door was closed and a blanket had been strung over the sole window. Unless Howard peeked out, he might make it undetected.

Dust got into his nostrils and he had to repress an urge to sneeze. Sweat trickled down his spine and his sides became clammy. A large leopard lizard popped out from under a bush to regard him hungrily, then retreated when it realized he was a bigger morsel than it cared to tackle.

The door remained closed.

The blanket over the window didn't move.

Skye felt as if his brain were being baked by the sun. His mouth was bone dry, his lips parched for moisture. His hat brim shielded his eyes from the worst of the glare but he still had to squint to see clearly. Mentally he ticked off the yards, his gaze glued to the window and the door.

He saw Howard's horse lift its head and look at him and he involuntarily stiffened. This was the moment of truth. He aimed at the window, ready to fire should Howard appear. To his immense relief the horse wasn't in the least bit concerned and lowered its head to nibble at some brown grass. He crawled faster.

From inside came muffled voices, a man and a woman's in heated argument.

Rosemary did live, then! Elated, he started to rise, intending to dash the last fifteen yards and crash through the door before Pete Howard knew what hit him. Suddenly the blanket over the window was moved aside and he flattened again, pressing the stock to his shoulder.

Framed in the opening was Rosemary. She saw him, her eyes widening in surprise but otherwise she maintained her composure and didn't betray his presence.

He rose into a crouch and hurried forward, counting on her to block Howard's view. When still seven yards or so from the cabin he heard a gruff voice from within.

"—doing there, anyway? Sit back down, bitch, or you'll be real sorry."

"I just wanted a little air," Rosemary said, and smiled wanly at Skye. She pulled the blanket over the window as she turned and disappeared.

Fargo reached the corner and squatted. If Howard kept talking he would be able to pinpoint the bastard's position and know which way to face after he kicked in the door. But neither of them was speaking.

"What do you intend to do with me?" Rosemary unexpectedly inquired.

There was a sigh of exasperation. "We've already been through this a dozen times," Howard declared gruffly.

"I'm taking you to Los Angeles with me and there isn't a damn thing you can do about it."

"I think you're lying. You have no intention of letting me live that long."

"Know it all, don't you?" Howard responded testily.

"You don't dare allow me to live to spread the word of what you've done."

"I haven't laid a finger on you," Howard said.

"Only because there hasn't been time," Rosemary said. "You've been too busy running from Slade and Fargo. But you took me against my will, you made me ride with you at gunpoint. If the word got around, you'd end your days swinging from a rope. Men out here don't take kindly to women being molested."

"You talk too much," Howard grumbled. "I'm beginning to think you're more trouble than you're worth. First you let Fargo's horse slip away, then you tried to escape last night, and the whole time you've been cackling worse than a bandy hen."

"I demand to be set free."

Howard laughed. "Demand all you want, missy. We're staying right here until dark. Once the sun sets, we'll ride for the California border. Now shut your mouth, woman, or you'll get me riled."

"I'm quaking in fear."

Fargo edged toward the door, impressed by Rosemary's courage. She was deliberately keeping Howard talking so the hard case wouldn't hear any slight noises outside. He paused under the window and glanced up at the green blanket, tempted to give it a good shove and blast away. But as near as he could tell, Pete Howard was near the southwest corner. He would have to poke the Sharps all the way in, lean over the sill, and twist sharply to fire, which would give Howard time to cut loose. Kicking in the door, on the other hand, might startle Howard enough that he would get the drop on him.

"Keep prodding me, bitch," Howard snapped. "I'll gut you here and now and leave you for the buzzards."

"Touch me and I'll scream."

Pete Howard laughed. "Be my guest. There isn't another soul within ten miles of here."

"What about the Paiutes?"

"We cut no Injun sign after leaving that valley. Those Paiutes are too busy chasing Rafe and that Trailsman feller, if they got out of there with their hides on, to bother us any."

"I'll scream anyway."

"Go right ahead."

Fargo sprang into motion the instant Rosemary shrieked. He took two bounds, grabbed the latch, and lifted as he threw his shoulder against the door. It swung inward on creaking hinges and he vaulted into the dusty room.

Pete Howard was on the right, lying on a blanket with a rifle by his side. Stunned, he stiffened, then reached for the gun.

In a single swift stride Fargo was there. His right foot flashed upward and caught Howard on the tip of the chin, mashing the man's yellow teeth together. Howard gurgled as blood spurted down over his chin, then he attempted to stand. But Fargo wasn't about to let him. Another kick landed full on Howard's mouth and the man slumped forward, his eyelids quivering, bleeding profusely. Taking a ragged breath, Howard tried to stand but passed out, slumping over on his side.

"You should have killed him," Rosemary said.

Skye turned. She stood near the window, a hand resting on the top of a rickety wooden table. "Not yet. I may get some use out of him later."

"In what way?"

"You'll see," Fargo said, and had to hold the Sharps to one side as she dashed into his arms and hugged him with all her might. He felt a tear moisten his cheek and her hot breath in his ear.

"Thank God you found us. I thought I'd never get to see San Francisco."

He curled an arm around her slender shoulders and heard her sniffle. "I would never have overtaken you if my pinto hadn't shown up when it did."

"He made me bring it along when we left, but I released the reins the first chance I had. It headed right back to the valley," Rosemary detailed, and chuckled. "Howard was fit to be tied."

"Last night I heard a shot?" Fargo mentioned.

"I tried to slip away when we stopped briefly to rest

the horses. He put a bullet into the ground at my feet to get me to stop."

Fargo felt her shudder.

"He was getting set to tie me up when I happened to look out the window," Rosemary said softly. "I've never been so happy in my whole damn life as when I saw you playing snake out front."

Lying on the table was a lariat. Fargo took it and bound Howard hand and foot. Then he hauled the hard case to the other side of the room and deposited him in a corner. "This will do until we leave."

Rosemary slapped a hand to her forehead. "In all the excitement of seeing you again I didn't think to ask. Did you find Lida?"

"She's holed up with Slade. He took a lance," Fargo replied, striding to the door. "We'll head back as soon as the sun sets."

"Why not now?"

"Because I was up all night and I'm exhausted," Fargo admitted. "If I don't get some shut-eye I'll fall asleep in the saddle. My horse can use some rest and water, too." He nodded at the rifle and pistol he'd taken from Howard and placed on the table. "Keep him covered until I get back."

"You're not leaving?" Rosemary asked anxiously.

"Just to fetch my pinto," Fargo assured her, and went out. The heat drilled into every pore, the brilliant sunshine seared his eyes. Hastening to the top of the ridge, he walked toward the sheltered cleft where he had left the Ovaro.

Out on the plain a pinpoint of light flared.

Fargo crouched and slid his thumbs over the rifle hammer. Someone was out there, perhaps a mile or more away. Had a war party found his tracks? Staying low, he ran to the stallion and mounted. Then, bending over the saddle horn to reduce his silhouette, he kept below the skyline and rode down to the cabin.

Rosemary, rifle in hand, waited near the open door. "I don't want you to leave me alone again," she said. "My nerves can't take the strain."

"You're doing fine," Fargo said, swinging off the stallion. "And you'll need steady nerves. I think we have company coming."

"Paiutes?"

"Don't know yet," Fargo responded, taking the stallion over to the tree where the other horses were tied.

Rosemary dogged his heels. "Shouldn't we run?"

"We wouldn't get very far with my horse as tired as it is, and yours isn't in much better shape. And I've been in the saddle for the better part of twenty-four hours," Fargo said, and nodded at the cabin. "No, I'll stay here and take my chances. If the Paiutes find us, this is as good a place as any to make a stand. At least we have water handy."

"I'd rather run."

Skye let the Ovaro drink its fill. He moved a few feet to the right, knelt, and sank his lips into the cold, delicious water, gulping as noisily as the pinto. Momentarily invigorated, he filled his canteen and slung it over his left shoulder.

"I'd really rather run," Rosemary reiterated, fidgeting nervously as she scanned the ridge.

"Trust me," Fargo said. He noticed there was a large patch of shade at the rear of the cabin and took the Ovaro there. He saw the heads of several large nails jutting an inch or more from the unpainted, slightly warped boards, and he tied the reins to one of them. He wished he dared strip his saddle and the *mochila* off the weary animal, but for all his talk about making a stand he knew they might need to ride on out in a hurry and he wanted the pinto handy. "Bring the other horses over," he directed.

As Rosemary complied, he scanned the top of the ridge but saw nothing to indicate anyone was up there. The Paiutes, though, wouldn't advertise their presence. When Rosemary returned he tied the reins of each to one of the nails, gave them a tug to verify they were held fast, and headed for the door.

"Don't you ever get worried?" Rosemary asked.

Fargo looked at her.

"I've yet to see you ruffled by anything," she elaborated. "You seem to take everything in stride. Even when you're fighting, you act as if it's the most natural thing in the world. You're never the least bit excited."

He ran his eyes up and down her full figure and smirked. "I wouldn't say that."

"You know what I mean. How do you do it?"

At the entrance Fargo paused to scour the terrain one more time. "Live in the wild long enough and you learn to accept whatever comes along. Look at an Indian. To him, fighting and death are just part of day-to-day living, as normal as breathing and eating. And since a man never knows when an arrow or a grizzly's claws might put an end to his life, he shouldn't lose any sleep worrying about it." He hefted the canteen. "When our time is up there isn't a damn thing we can do about it."

"I know all that, but in my heart I also know I'd make a rotten rancher's wife. I could never accept Indian raids and wild beasts as normal life. I'd worry myself into an early grave."

Fargo motioned for her to enter first, then trailed. He deposited the Sharps and the canteen on the table and glanced at Pete Howard.

The weasel was awake and sitting up, his eyes blazing hatred. His lips were pulp and two of his front teeth were chipped badly. Blood caked his mouth and chin. "I'll kill you for this, you son of a bitch," he growled, grimacing from the pain.

"Didn't expect you to come around so soon. You must have a head like a rock," Fargo commented, moving to Howard's blanket and taking a seat. "Nice blanket you've got here."

"I'll gut you and stake you out to die."

"Big words for a man trussed up like a steer for the slaughter," Fargo said. "You figuring on gnawing through those ropes and jumping me when I'm not looking? I didn't know you were part beaver."

Rosemary snickered.

"Have your fun, bastards," Howard said, and lapsed into sullen silence.

"What do we do now?" Rosemary asked, lifting the blanket to peer out the window.

"Wait."

"That's all?"

"Yep." Fargo lay back and braced his head on his hands, calculating the risk he was taking. If there were Paiutes on his trail they would show up in an hour or so. Fleeing, with the horses in the condition they were in, would be useless. The Paiutes would catch them easily, and they might find themselves surrounded somewhere out in the open where they wouldn't have a prayer. He stuck by his original decision to make a stand at the cabin should the need arise. "Wake me in about an hour," he directed, closing his eyes.

"You're going to *sleep* at a time like this?"

Fargo didn't answer. His lack of rest finally took its toll and fatigue washed over him like the rushing waters of a rain-swollen river over their banks. One moment he dimly heard Rosemary's voice. The next his mind was swamped by a wave of black emptiness and he heard nothing at all.

The pressure of something on his shoulder awakened him instantly and he sat bolt upright, his right hand automatically falling to his Colt. "What is it?" he asked, aware of the sweat on his body and the buzzing of a fly somewhere in the cabin.

Rosemary was crouched at his side. "Men are coming."

"Indians?"

"No. White men."

Puzzled, Fargo shook his head to dispel the lingering cobwebs of sleep and stood. He crossed to the window and found Rosemary had used a piece of old string to tie up one end. Bending down, he stared out at the parched landscape.

Something moved, perhaps a hundred and fifty yards out. From behind the mesquite appeared two men on horseback, then two more. They were eyeing the cabin and discussing their next move. All four held rifles.

"Outlaws, maybe?" Rosemary asked.

"Don't know," Fargo said, picking up the Sharps. He fed a cartridge in and thumbed back the hammer.

Pete Howard had sat up. "If they're pards of mine they'll skin you alive," he boasted.

"Not before I blow your brains out," Fargo told him, and shifted his attention to Rosemary. "How long was I asleep?"

"Forty minutes by my watch."

Not anywhere near enough, Fargo reflected, regretting his decision to rest. He felt like crap. His muscles ached, his joints were stiff, and his mind was sluggish. Another eight or ten hours of heavy slumber would make a new man of him, but he held no hope of enjoying any extended rest until he reached California. *If* he reached California.

The four riders were approaching the cabin, fanning out as they did. In the middle rode a burly man wearing a flannel shirt and a brown hat. He seemed to be issuing instructions to the others, who spread out according to his directions.

Skye waited until they were seventy yards out, then cupped a hand to his mouth and shouted, "That's far enough!"

The quartet halted and engaged in an animated conversation. Eventually the burly one replied.

"We're friendly, mister! We'd like a drink from your spring, if you don't mind."

"Just one of you come on in," Fargo ordered. "The rest hang back until I say it's all right." He saw the burly man say something and start forward. "I'm going out," he informed Rosemary. "Keep me covered but don't show yourself. Just stick the rifle barrel out so they can see it."

Nodding, she moved to the opening and poked Howard's rifle into the sunlight.

Fargo cradled the Sharps in the crook of his left arm, leaving his right hand free to employ the Colt if necessary, and strode a few yards to the left of the door. The burly man glanced from him to the rifle barrel at the window, then back again.

"Howdy, stranger. Where's Tad Wilcox?"

"Don't know the man," Fargo replied.

"That's sort of peculiar," the burly rider stated, leaning forward. "This being his cabin, and all."

"There was no one at home when I got here," Fargo said. "This Wilcox a friend of yours?"

"Not particularly. My name is Carl Weatherford, and I'm a miner out of Virginia City. So are the rest of these boys," Weatherford said, twisting to indicate his companions. "We were sort of elected to go out and check on folks who hadn't been heard from since the Injun trouble commenced."

"Elected?" Fargo said.

Weatherford cracked a grin. "They took a vote of all the miners at the Comstock Saloon. Us four were so drunk we couldn't object when some of the others picked us and put it to a vote."

"You're taking a big risk," Fargo commented. "There are Paiute war parties all over this territory."

"Don't we know it!" Weatherford replied. "We've been hiding from them off and on for the past six days." He frowned and removed his hat to slap thick dust from his shirt and pants. "Haven't found a living soul yet, either. Every Express station east of Lake Tahoe is either deserted or been burned to the ground. There were a bunch of dead settlers at Honey Lake, a party of eight who were killed about sixty miles from there, and a couple more on the Truckee River. Those damn Paiutes are thorough, I can tell you that."

"I've seen some of their handiwork."

Weatherford nodded at the cabin. "I slung the bull with old Tad a few times back in Virginia City and knew he was prospecting in these parts. Figured we'd come here before calling it quits and heading back to Virginia City." He replaced his hat. "I don't mind telling you we're plumb tuckered out."

"Have your friends ride on in," Fargo said, relaxing. He'd met enough miners in his time to know Carl Weatherford was the genuine article and not likely to be a friend of Pete Howard's. "Water your horses at the spring and we'll get some coffee started."

The burly miner stared at the rifle barrel jutting from the window. "You're not one for taking chances, are you?"

"I like breathing," Fargo said, and turned to the door.

"Didn't catch your handle, mister."

"Fargo. Skye Fargo."

Weatherford blinked. "Do tell. Well, I'm right pleased to meet you, sir." Wheeling his mount, he rode out to inform the others.

Skye stepped inside. "You can lean the rifle against the wall for now," he told Rosemary. "These men won't be a problem." Going back outside, he walked around the cabin and took his saddlebags from the Ovaro. "I'll rub you down soon," he promised, giving the stallion a pat on the neck.

As he came around the front corner the four miners were drawing rein. All four still held their rifles, and he thought nothing of it as he stopped and held up his saddlebags. "I have some fine coffee in here. We'll have a pot boiling in no time."

"Awful neighborly of you," Weatherford said, then added swiftly, "Now!"

Suddenly Skye Fargo found himself looking down four long, dark barrels and heard the clicks of four hammers being pulled back.

"One move and you're dead," Weatherford said.

# 13

Fargo turned to stone, the Sharps held next to his right leg, the muzzle pointed downward. He felt certain the four men would riddle him with slugs if he so much as lifted the rifle a hair. They had taken him completely unawares. His only hope was that Rosemary had heard and would open fire from the window, a hope dashed to bits the very next instant.

"Say. What's the meaning of this?"

Rosemary was framed in the doorway, her hands on her hips, staring in shocked disbelief at the quartet. "I thought you were friendly."

Carl Weatherford sneered. "We'll be as friendly as can be to you, lady," he said.

"Where did she come from?" asked the skinniest of the bunch.

"Who cares about her?" retorted another. "Where's Pete? We know that's his horse out back."

From inside the cabin came a triumphant cackle. "I'm in here, boys, trussed up. One of you cut me loose pronto."

The skinny rider climbed down and hurried inside.

"Fooled you, didn't we?" Weatherford said to Fargo.

"Slick as could be," Skye admitted, staying still as one of the others swung to the ground and came over to strip him of the Sharps and the Colt. The man checked around his waist for a second revolver but didn't think to search in his boots.

"Not your fault," Weatherford said when the searcher backed off. "We really are miners. Or I should say we *were* until we saw the light. All four of us came west about half a year ago thinking we'd become wealthy in no time. We'd all heard about the rich ore being scooped out of the ground in Carson County."

The searcher snorted. "Rich ore, hell! All we ever dug up was dirt and more dirt."

"And that was our problem, you see," Weatherford went on. "We were all flat busted with no prospect of ever striking it rich since all the good claims had already been staked out."

Fargo listened patiently, biding his time. Sooner or later they might drop their guard, giving him an opportunity to grab the toothpick.

"We were about to call it quits and head back to the States with our tails tucked between our legs when we ran into Rafe Slade and Pete Howard," Weatherford revealed. "Pete started us to thinking on how we might come out ahead of the game."

"I'll bet," Fargo said. He knew all about the hundreds and hundreds of men who had flocked to Carson County after word of the first silver strike went out. Most were still there, living in tents, crude huts, or even caves as they hunted for the glittering ore they were convinced would make them millionaires. And more greedy sorts just like them were arriving every day, or had been until the stage service was disrupted by the Paiute war.

"With the Injuns on a killing spree and scaring most everyone else out of the country, this area is wide open," Weatherford said. "Pete figures we can hit a few ranches and steal them blind, and maybe the few Express stations that haven't been destroyed. There's bound to be valuables, even if the folks have pulled out. The Paiutes will get all the blame. And when we reach Salt Lake City we should each wind up with a stake of at least a couple of hundred dollars."

So now Skye knew why the two hard cases had been in the area. But a couple of questions remained. "Did the four of you get separated from Howard and Slade?"

"Yep," Weatherford answered. "A band of—."

"Shut your damn mouth!" Pete Howard roared, bursting from the cabin and storming up to Weatherford's mount. "You never known when to keep that gabby mouth of your closed, do you, idiot?"

"All I—," Weatherford began.

"Spare me your lame excuses," Howard snapped. "You always talk too much for your own good." Spinning, he pointed at Fargo. "I want him tied up for the time being. I have plans for this son of a bitch, but first things first." His crafty gaze strayed from Skye to Rosemary and he licked his lips. "Yes, sir. Plans like you wouldn't believe."

"Touch a hair on her head and you'll be hung," Fargo quickly came to her defense.

"By who? You? No one else will ever know," Howard gloated. "I can do as I damn well please."

"What about these men?" Fargo asked, gesturing at the miners. "They've lived by the law most of their lives, until they hooked up with you. Are they going to stand by and do nothing while you force yourself on this woman?" He saw the miners share troubled expressions and knew he'd planted a seed of doubt and distrust in their minds.

"You never said anything about molesting women," Carl Weatherford addressed Howard.

"Yeah," added one of the others. "I don't like the notion of hurting a lady."

Howard glared at both of them. "And what did you reckon would happen if we hit a ranch where the folks were still there? We'd maybe water our horses and politely ride away?" He shook his head. "All of you agreed to this deal before we left Virginia City. You all knew what you were getting into."

"There was never any talk of rape," Weatherford said distastefully, refusing to be intimidated. "Robbing was all we discussed."

Howard's right hand drifted near his empty holster. His fingers brushed the leather and he did a double take as if realizing he was unarmed.

"If you're thinking of touching this woman, we have to talk some more," added the skinny man.

"Fine," Howard spat in disgust. "We'll talk ourselves blue in the faces. In the meantime, I thought I said I want Fargo tied up. Just like I was so he has no chance of getting away."

Skye was escorted inside where the skinny miner and one with a pockmarked face used the same lengths of rope he had used to bind Howard and securely bound him by the wrists and the ankles. Left alone, he leaned against the wall and listened while the miners attended to their horses. Weatherford and Howard spent most of the time arguing. He glimpsed Rosemary standing outside, but she made no move to enter until told to do so by Pete Howard.

"Make us some coffee and fix some grub," the outlaw directed. He had reclaimed his pistol and rifle and carried himself with an arrogant swagger.

The four miners filed inside, each appearing uncomfortable and nervous, and took seats at various points. Carl Weatherford sat down near Skye.

"After we eat we'll head for a ranch southeast of here," Howard informed them. "Should get there about dawn."

"What about Rafe Slade?" asked the skinny miner.

"He's gone his own way," Howard replied. "We hooked up with this woman here and another, and Rafe went and fell for the other one."

"Tell them the truth," Fargo prompted.

Pete Howard pivoted and crouched like a coiling sidewinder, his gun hand poised to draw. "Not a word out of you, mister, or I'll finish it right now."

"Hold on," Weatherford said, glancing at Skye. "What are you getting at?"

It was Rosemary who answered before Howard could stop her. "My friend, Lida, was taken by the Paiutes. Fargo and Rafe went into a Paiute village after her, and while they were gone Howard rode off with their horses and forced me to go with him."

A somber silence prevailed. The miners cast accusing gazes at Howard, who shifted his stance and hefted his rifle.

"What do you have to say for yourself?" Weatherford demanded at last.

"Whose word are you going to take?" Howard rejoined. "Hers or mine? She's lying because she's stuck on Fargo and wants both of them to get out of here alive."

"You're planning to kill her?" the pockmarked miner asked, his tone reflecting his estimation of anyone who would murder a woman.

Fargo seized the moment. If he could turn the miners against Howard, he might be able to get himself and Rosemary out of the fix they were in without resorting to gunplay. "Of course he is, boys." Inspiration struck and he took a calculated gamble. "Killing women is second nature to a bastard like Howard. He's done it before."

Pete Howard hissed and took a stride, his hand falling to his pistol. "Liar! Damn your hide! I should have rubbed you out when I had the chance."

The four miners lunged to their feet, Weatherford blocking Howard's view of Fargo. None of them spoke. They didn't have to. Their faces betrayed their feelings.

Pete Howard clearly didn't like what he saw. He backed up until he bumped into the table, then wiped his hand across his mouth. "What's gotten into you gents? I never killed no woman, and that's the gospel. Fargo is lying to save his skin."

"Funny thing," the skinny miner said. "I just remembered hearing about a man at a mining camp up in Oregon who shot and killed a saloon girl who wouldn't have anything to do with him." He cocked his head and inspected Howard from head to toe. "Now that I think of it, you match the description to the letter."

"Now hold on, Ogden," Howard said, adopting a lopsided grin. "I ain't never been up to Oregon so don't go accusing me of something I never done."

"Back in Virginia City you told me you had been to Oregon," Weatherford declared.

In a move that caught his accusers off guard, Howard sprang to the doorway and leveled his rifle, sweeping it from miner to miner. "The first man who lifts a weapon dies," he growled, easing farther out. "I can see that riding with a bunch of yellowbellies like you will get me nowhere, so I'm taking my leave. Don't interfere or some of you will eat lead." With that he whirled and dashed off.

"Should we go after him?" Ogden asked Weatherford.

"What for? We don't have any proof he was the one killed that gal up in Oregon."

"You know he did as well as I do," Ogden said.

"Maybe so. But I don't feel like going out there and getting myself killed by that son of a bitch when he'll be out of our hair in a minute or two," Weatherford replied, and glanced at Rosemary. "Besides, I figure we've made enough mistakes the past couple of weeks and I don't want to make any more."

"Then cut me loose," Fargo spoke up, holding his arms up.

"If we do, I want your word you won't hold this against us," Weatherford said. "I want for all four of us to ride away without any trouble."

Fargo had no reason to object. He hadn't been harmed and Rosemary was now safe. "You have my word," he said, then faced the door at the sound of shuffling footsteps.

Everyone else did the same.

Pete Howard appeared, walking slowly, unsteadily, his arms limp at his sides, his rifle dangling loosely from his right hand. His eyes were wide with fright. He tried to speak, his lips trembling from the effort, but all that came out was a trickle of blood from the corner of his mouth.

"What the hell!" one of the miners blurted.

Howard took another shuffling step, his left hand starting to rise. There was a loud thud and he suddenly stumbled into the jamb, his rifle falling from his limp fingers. He glanced at Rosemary and tried to reach for her. Suddenly there was a second thud. Howard arched his back, staggered, and fell to his knees. "Help—!" he croaked, then pitched onto his face.

Three arrows jutted from his back.

"Damn!" a miner bellowed, and stepped to the entrance with his rifle tight against his shoulder.

"Don't!" Fargo tried to warn the man, but even as he did an arrow streaked out of the bright sky and struck the miner full in the chest. The man clutched at the shaft, stumbled, and sprawled over Pete Howard's body.

Finally the remaining miners galvanized into action. "It's the Paiutes!" Weatherford bellowed. "We've got to close the door!" With the help of his friends he succeeded in hauling Howard and the dead miner inside and shutting it.

Ogden moved to the window and peeked out. "I don't see anyone."

"They're out there," Weatherford said, staring sadly at the slain miner. "If you show yourself you'll wind up like Howard and Goff."

Rosemary had backed against the rear wall, her hand

over her throat. "What will we do?" she asked of no one in particular.

"The first thing is for someone to cut me the hell loose!" Fargo said impatiently, wagging his hands. He dreaded what would happen if the Paiutes should rush the cabin and overpower the miners before he was freed. The braves would have him at their mercy; they would torture him for days, prolonging the agony as long as possible, then leave him for the buzzards.

"Here," Weatherford said to Rosemary while pulling a butcher knife from a sheath on his left hip. "You do the honors. We must keep watch."

She dashed to Skye's side, knelt, and applied the cutting edge to the ropes. In short order she had his wrists loose, then his ankles.

"Thanks," Fargo said, pushing to his feet. He stepped to the table where his Colt and Sharps lay and picked up both. Weatherford and Ogden were on either side of the window. The other miner had an ear to the door.

"Do we make a run for it?" Rosemary asked.

"No," Skye answered. "We wouldn't get ten feet. We'll have to wait for dark."

"What about the horses?" Ogden wondered.

Skye had been worried about the same thing from the moment he heard the arrow strike Howard. The Paiutes would have rounded up the stock at the spring and driven them off first thing. But there was a slim possibility the warriors hadn't noticed the three horses directly behind the cabin, or if they had they hadn't tried to take them for fear of being shot at.

He moved to the back wall and examined the boards carefully. Tad Wilcox had constructed his ramshackle home from old, weatherworn lumber probably packed in on mules from Virginia City. Most of the boards were warped, many cracked. None had ever been painted. And there were thin openings between several, the result of Wilcox's shoddy workmanship. A typical prospector, Wilcox had rushed completing the cabin so he could devote his time to finding gold. Rare was the prospector who bothered to construct a permanent dwelling place.

"What are you up to?" Weatherford inquired.

"We can't see the spring or the back of the cabin from the window," Fargo mentioned. He took the butcher knife from Rosemary, leaned the Sharps in a corner, and began digging into a narrow slit, widening it.

"Good thinking," Ogden said. "We can cover the rear and keep the savages from setting fire to the place."

"Do you think they will?" Rosemary asked, aghast.

"They're crafty devils," Ogden said. "Don't put anything past them."

It took several minutes for Fargo to carve out a hole large enough to see clearly. Outside all was still. Perhaps the Paiutes figured to wait them out, to sit tight until they ran out of water and food. The heat would drive them outdoors eventually where the war party would be waiting. And since the Paiutes had access to the spring, the braves would be rested and refreshed when the final fight came.

The first sight he saw on peeking through the hole was the Ovaro munching on a cluster of brown grass. Turning his head, he also spied Rosemary's mount and Howard's horse. He had to tilt his neck to glimpse the spring, which lay about twenty yards from the northeast corner. The miners had picketed their horses there, and the animals were now gone. Lying on the ground, drinking heartily, was a Paiute brave. Four more stood nearby eyeing the three horses at the back of the cabin.

Fargo set to work with the knife again. The Paiutes had figured out they could approach the rear of the cabin without being seen. Soon they would make their bid for the Ovaro and the other two mounts. He must discourage them.

"Are our horses still there?" Carl Weatherford asked.

"Afraid not."

"Damn it all," Weatherford muttered. "How will we get out of here without horses? It's too far to Virginia City to try and make it on foot."

The sharp knife bit deep into the wood, sending the chips flying as Fargo twisted and gouged. The hole widened, becoming large enough to accommodate the barrel of the Sharps. He continued to enlarge it. The bigger it was, the better angle he would have for a shot. When the hole was two inches in size he paused and peered outside once more.

Those four warriors were slinking toward the cabin.

He placed the tip of the barrel into the hole, shifted

so the Sharps was pointing in their general directions, and inserted a cartridge. He didn't expect to hit much since he couldn't see to aim clearly, but the shot should prevent them from making another try for the horses any time soon. Squinting, he gazed along the barrel and just barely saw the skulking warriors. The hole needed to be even larger but he didn't have the time. He waited until a brave seemed to be in a direct line of fire, and fired.

At the booming retort the Paiutes reacted like jackrabbits and bounded off into the brush. All except for one. He spun, clutched at his shoulder, then jogged for cover.

"Did you nail one?" Weatherford inquired.

"Winged one," Fargo disclosed, feeding another cartridge into his rifle. Until dark, at least, the three horses would be safe. Then the Paiutes would likely try again.

Rosemary was kneeling at the crude stone fireplace, assembling dry twigs and branches. She had already poured water from the canteen into his coffeepot and added some coffee grounds.

"There's one!" Ogden cried, lifting his rifle. He paused, then cursed. "The buck ran to ground."

Weatherford leaned on the wall and looked at Skye. "You're supposed to be a topnotch Indian fighter. What's our best bet?"

"To sit tight until dark. Then we'll make our break and try to reach the top of the ridge. If we gain the high ground we might be able to hold them off."

"Without enough horses we won't get far."

The man had a point. There were three mounts and five of them. Riding double would do for a while but the animals couldn't go any great distance bearing extra weight. A crazy idea occurred to him and he shook his head to dispel it. Talk about certain suicide. Yet it was the only means of possibly getting all of them out of there alive. He pondered the situation at length during the long hours that dragged past as if weighted with anchors, enjoying two cups of steaming brew in the process.

Ogden and the other miner spoke little. They took turns at the window, each eager for a shot that never came. The Paiutes were invisible, blending into the landscape as naturally as rocks and brush.

Carl Weatherford jabbered a great deal, mostly to Rosemary. They talked about the silver strike in Carson

County and the gold strike back Denver way, about his life as a hardscrabble farmer before he came to the West in search of his fortune, and about the wonders of California neither had yet seen.

Toward evening Rosemary passed around pieces of jerked venison to serve as their supper. She nibbled on hers, her appetite supplanted by a knot of fear in her gut.

The sun hovered above the western horizon when Fargo made up his mind. He had moved to the window and lifted the edge of the blanket to scour the terrain. How many Paiutes were out there? he mused. Ten? Twenty? Any more than that and he wouldn't stand a prayer.

"I have a plan," he announced.

"Let's hear it," Weatherford responded.

So Skye briefly outlined his brainstorm, and when he concluded their skepticism was obvious.

"You're asking to lose your hair," Ogden said. "No white man can beat them at their own game."

"If we stay put we're all dead," Fargo pointed out. "Our water won't last another day. Three days from now we'll be so thirsty we'd drink mud. And without much food we'll grow weaker and weaker until the damned Paiutes can waltz in here and take our guns from our hands without a struggle." He regarded each of them. "Is that what you want to happen?"

"Of course not," Weatherford said. "Your idea is downright loco, but I reckon it's the only hope we have."

"Just keep an eye on the horses out back," Fargo instructed him. "If the Paiutes sneak in and get those, my plan is shot to hell."

"What will the signal be?" Weatherford asked.

Fargo thought for a moment. "Three quick shots in a row. You won't have much time so come out the door on the run. I'll hold up my end."

Rosemary came over and touched his arm. "It seems like I'm forever telling you to be careful. Make it back, please."

Nodding, Fargo stepped to the door and made certain he had a round in the Sharps. "Remember. No shooting unless you hear me fire first. I doubt all of the braves are watching the cabin. Most are likely sitting around talking or getting set for their evening meal while the rest have us surrounded." He drew his Colt. "Any shooting will draw the whole band."

"I still think it would be safer for you to wait until the sun sets," Weatherford suggested.

"They'd expect that. And after dark it'll be easier for them to steal our remaining horses," Fargo said, checking the cylinder. "No, this way is better."

"I hope to hell you know what you're doing," Weatherford replied.

"So do I," Fargo said, and yanked the door wide. With the Colt in one hand and the Sharps in the other he darted from the safety of the cabin, exposing himself to the hostile eyes of the waiting warriors.

# 14

Skye counted on the swiftness of the act to momentarily catch the Paiutes off guard. He cut to the left along the cabin, bending at the waist and running as fast as his legs would carry him, and he was almost to the corner when he heard the door close and the first arrow flashed out of nowhere and smacked into the wood within inches of his face. Skirting the quivering shaft, he raced around the corner toward the rear.

Most of the Paiutes, he figured, would be west of the cabin so they could watch the door and the window. Only a few would be keeping an eye on the three horses, and they would have no idea he was outside until he came around the back corner. A loud whoop pierced the air from out front as he took the second corner on the fly.

The Ovaro looked up.

Angry yells and fierce cries erupted all around as Fargo reached his horse and vaulted into the saddle. He tugged the reins loose from the nail, still holding the rifle and the Colt, and put his spurs to the pinto as he slanted to the south.

A lone Paiute materialized from behind a rock, a bow in his hands.

Fargo snapped off a shot, the Colt blasting and bucking. A red-rimmed hole blossomed in the warrior's forehead and he toppled.

Two more braves popped up from concealment, one armed with a lance, the other a bow.

Riding low over the saddle, barely able to grip the reins with the same hand that held the Sharps, Fargo aimed at the bowman and fired, then swiveled and fired at the other Paiute as the man heaved the lance. He slid onto the side of the pinto, holding on for dear life with one palm and one heel, and swore he could feel a slight rush of air as the lance flashed by an inch above the Ovaro's neck.

Then he reached the sparse brush and swung upright. A frenzy of shouts testified to how the war party felt about his impending escape. He kept to a straight course, glancing over his shoulder every few seconds until he saw a band of nine or ten braves in bloodthirsty pursuit. Good. This would reduce the odds considerably when he returned to get Rosemary and the miners out of there. If he returned.

Fargo stayed near the ridge, seeking a means of reaching the top. The combination of sheer walls and talus slopes thwarted his intent, and the farther he went from the cabin the slimmer became the likelihood of his plan working. He must get up there where a network of ravines, clusters of boulders, and scattered hills would enable him to elude the Paiutes.

The cabin was no longer in sight.

He shoved the Sharps into the scabbard but kept the Colt out for ready use. A finger of talus forced him to swing farther out from the ridge than he would have liked, and sure enough the Paiutes used the fleeting detour to reduce the gap. They were shrieking like madmen, anxious to kill him, most with arrows already notched to their bows.

For a mile the chase continued with the Ovaro holding its own. Fargo spotted a break up ahead but he couldn't tell if it was a way of gaining the rim. Hunched over, he galloped to within ten yards of the opening before discovering a narrow, gravel-strewn grade leading to his destination.

Without hesitation he cut into the opening and began the arduous climb. The loose gravel underfoot made treacherous going for the pinto but the big stallion was, as ever, game to the core. Up it went, hoofs flying, struggling to find a firm purchase, losing more ground to the gaining Paiutes.

Fargo glanced over his left shoulder. The band was nearly in effective pistol range. He raised his arm, sighting deliberately, and squeezed off the shot. Seventy yards out a brave clutched at his torso and fell under the flailing hoofs of the mounts ringing him. The Paiutes broke, about half angling away from the ridge while the rest stayed on their original course. The tactic was simple, as old as time itself. A lone man couldn't possibly hold off overwhelming numbers bearing down from more than one direction. The Paiutes knew it and Skye knew it, too.

He didn't waste more ammunition trying to slow them down. Instead, he focused exclusively on attaining the rim, a haven that might as well be in another territory for all the good it would do him until he was up there. The Ovaro's hoofs pounded and clattered, and loose gravel and rocks rattled down the slope. He was halfway up before he looked at the Indians again.

The Paiutes had slowed near the bottom of the grade. None of them dared to ride onto the grade since they would be right out in the open, easy targets.

He smiled, imagining their frustration. Then he saw the majority in both groups lift their bows and his skin crawled at the thought of what was coming. "Hyyyy-aaahh!" he yelled, goading the Ovaro, but the stallion was doing its utmost and could do no more.

From the rear came the twang of seven bowstrings being released in unison. From below swept the hiss of arrows in flight, a hiss that grew louder and louder to culminate in a lethal downpour of whizzing shafts.

Fargo involuntarily flinched as several of the arrows arced past him, barely missing. Startled, the Ovaro whinnied and almost lost its footing. He held the reins firmly and coaxed the horse higher. "You can do it!" he declared. "You can do it!"

The rattle of hoofs below caused Skye to turn in the saddle. A pair of warriors had thrown caution to the proverbial wind and were sweeping up the grade after him. Both held lances. They had to get close to employ their weapons, unlike the bowmen who could fire from a distance, and they were clearly determined to do so.

He leveled the Colt and fired from the hip, palming the trigger back twice in swift succession, the hammering of the shots making one echo. Both warriors were hurled backwards to tumble off the back ends of their steeds and crash onto the rocky slope. No one would try that again for a minute or so, he reflected, and threw himself into the climb with renewed vigor.

The crest was on him in a rush and he drew rein

sharply. Ahead stretched a series of ravines. To his left, in the distance, hills. On his right reared monolithic boulders. He galloped toward the nearest ravine, stopped, and swung down to rip a waist-high bush out by the roots. Whirling back and forth, he brushed the bush over the dry ground, raising a cloud of dust that hopefully would fool the Paiutes into thinking he had entered the ravine. By the time they realized their mistake it would be too late.

He cast the bush off to one side and swung into the saddle, then rode behind a boulder near the crest. None too soon. As he pulled on the reins he heard the thunder of hoofs and over the top surged the Paiutes. A leading brave spotted the dust cloud at the ravine mouth and shouted an exclamation. In a mass the band poured into the ravine and was swallowed by the cloud.

Got you! Fargo was elated, and again spurred the Ovaro. He took the grade at a reckless gait, which couldn't be helped. Reaching the cabin before the band awoke to the trick was imperative. Rosemary's life and the lives of those miners depended on speed.

He made the return ride in almost the same amount of time he took on his desperate gambit, and he didn't allow the pinto to slow until the cabin came into sight. Then he took to the mesquite and cautiously worked his way to within a few hundred yards of the front door. Now came the hard part. He surveyed the countryside and spied three braves who were well hidden, watching the cabin.

Where were their horses? He had to sweep the surrounding terrain twice before he detected a flicker of movement approximately four hundred yards off, at the base of the ridge. Exercising all the skill at his command he rode in a loop until he was concealed in a gully and could observe the six war horses as the animals grazed on patches of sparse grass. The Paiutes, confident they had the whites pinned down, hadn't bothered to post a guard.

He took a prudent moment to replace the spent cartridges in the Colt, then squared his shoulders and rode up out of the gully on the run. A couple of the Indian mounts shied away at his approach, but he was still able to scoop up the rope reins on three of the horses and head them toward the cabin before the Paiutes perceived his strategy.

Furious yells punctuated the brush. Several of the Paiutes broke cover and converged from different directions.

Fargo wished he had another revolver or had decided on another signal. Say, two shots instead of three. Because now he expended half of the cartridges in his revolver as he fired a trio of shots to alert Rosemary and the miners.

The element of surprise worked in his favor. He was in the open and galloping up to the door before the first of the warriors burst from behind mesquite and brought a rifle to bear. The Colt cracked a fraction before the warrior could fire and the Paiute fell.

Out of the cabin rushed Weatherford, Ogden, and the third miner, providing covering fire for Skye, Rosemary in their wake. Weatherford and Ogden, according to plan, ran around the corner to fetch the two horses out back. The third miner stood in front of Rosemary, shielding her body with his own, and worked his rifle as rapidly as humanly possible.

Another Paiute ate dust.

Out of the corner of Skye's eye he saw a hefty brave throw back a brawny arm to heave a lance, and his shot was a shade too slow. The tip of the lance glistened as it flew like the beak of a giant bird of prey and sliced into the third miner's abdomen, ripping out his navel and tearing through his spine. The hapless man staggered, gripped the stout shaft, and looked at Skye in helpless appeal. Then the minor died, the inner light fading from his eyes as he sank with a sigh.

"Get on!" Fargo bellowed, gesturing with the rope reins.

Rosemary bounded to the nearest Indian pony, grasped its mane, and forked its back.

He had his hands full keeping the Paiutes at bay. Twice he snapped shots to force braves to seek shelter. Only one good cartridge remained in the revolver when Weatherford and Ogden galloped around the side of the cabin. Together, they sped for the ridge as bullets and arrows whistled on their heels. Skye held onto the extra horses to reduce the number of Paiutes who would be able to give chase.

To his surprise, no sign of pursuit was evident even after they had climbed to the ridge. Nor did he see a dust cloud over their back trail before the gathering twilight transformed into a moonless night. Eventually he called a halt in a tree-rimmed wash.

"Thank God," Rosemary said wearily, sliding down. "I thought for sure we were goners."

"You and me both, missy," Weatherford said, and glanced at Fargo. "Mister, you saved our bacon back there. We're in your debt. If you ever need a helping hand you say the word."

"The same goes for me," Ogden said.

"Obliged," Fargo responded, "but I just did what I had to." He grinned. "And you should always be careful how you say thanks to a man."

"Why's that?" Weatherford asked.

"Because as it so happens I can use your help."

"We meant what we said," Ogden responded. "We may be no-accounts in the eyes of those highfalutin types who prance around in their fancy carriages and live in homes the size of some barns, but our word is as good as the next man's. So have at it."

"Are both of you willing to do what you can to get Slade and Lida to safety?"

"Try us," Weatherford said.

"I will. Tomorrow," Skye promised, and moved the Ovaro to a grassy tract bordering a dry spring so the pinto could eat its full. He swiftly removed the saddle and the *mochila*, then gave the stallion a thorough rubdown using handfuls of grass. Afterwards, he let the Ovaro roll and pounded a picket pin into the earth.

The others had been busily attending to the rest of the horses. Weatherford finished first and walked over. "Cold camp tonight, I take it?"

"Yeah. Too risky to try even a small fire."

"Should we take turns on guard duty?"

Fargo nodded. "We'll need plenty of rest for what's in store. You take three hours, have Ogden take three hours, and I'll pull the last shift."

"Will do," Weatherford said, turning to go. "And Fargo, thanks again."

Stepping over to where he had deposited his gear at

the base of a tree, Fargo went to sit down. Soft footsteps stopped him short.

"Mind some company, big man?"

Rosemary came right up to him and put both hands on his shoulders. An impish grin curled her voluptuous lips. "I have my own way of saying thanks."

"Not tonight."

"You're joking, right? I haven't met the man yet who can refuse me."

"You have now," Skye told her, and turned to pick up his bedroll. "I haven't had a good night's sleep in more days than I care to remember. I've been in the saddle or fighting almost the whole time. And at first light it starts all over again." He stifled a yawn. "Tonight I need my rest."

"All right. If you insist. But at least let me sleep by your side. Without a fire it's going to get cold as a cow's teat on a winter morning."

"What about them?" Fargo asked, nodding at the spot a dozen yards off where Carl Weatherford was checking his rifle and Ogden was spreading his bedding.

"They can snuggle with their horses for all I care," Rosemary said. "I want your buns next to mine."

"And you'll behave?"

"On my honor," Rosemary said, her features shrouded in the inky shadows.

Resigned to sharing his blanket, Fargo moved off to a secluded spot where mesquite formed a barrier against the wind on three sides. After spreading the ground sheet and his blanket he sank down and tugged off his boots. The cool breeze tingled his feet.

Rosemary knelt and fiddled with her lustrous hair. "I'm a mess. I just know it. If we don't find a place to spruce up before we reach California I'll die from embarrassment."

"You?"

"Why not me?" Rosemary demanded. "You don't think ladies in my profession can have a sense of modesty?"

"Let me put it this way," Fargo responded, trying to be tactful. "Most of the fallen doves I've known have been more interested in taking their clothes off than in keeping them on."

"Which has nothing at all to do with genuine modesty. A woman can be stark naked and still be reserved and conduct herself like a proper lady."

Skye coughed to cover a budding laugh. An image flashed unbidden of rows of reserved and proper church-going ladies standing naked as plucked jaybirds in their pews. Somehow he couldn't see it. "Whatever you say," he replied. "I'm too bushed to debate the point. Now let's get some shut-eye."

He reclined on his back and placed the Sharps on his right side within easy reach. Rosemary stepped over him, the hem of her dress softly rubbing his face, and lay down on his left, putting her head on his shoulder.

"Isn't this nice?" she asked.

"Forget it. Go to sleep."

"Forget what? All I want to do is sleep."

"Care to make a bet?" Fargo asked, and felt a premonition when she didn't bother to reply. Closing his eyes, he listened to the breeze in the undergrowth and off to the west the familiar yipping of a lonely coyote. His body seemed to separate itself from his conscious mind and melt into nothingness of its own accord. Fingers touched his cheek, and that was the last thing he remembered until with amazement he felt a hand inside his britches, expertly fondling his manhood.

How long had he been asleep? He still was sore and tired and not at all inclined to let Rosemary indulge her raging hormones. To annoy her he kept his eyes closed and feigned heavy breathing. Her hand, however, paid no attention. And his pole, traitor that it was, had leaped to attention under her warm ministrations.

"I know you're awake," she whispered.

"No I'm not."

"Here you've been telling me one thing while your body is obviously interested in something else. What should we do about it?"

"Go to sleep. That's what I'm going to do."

"Care to make a bet?"

"I'm warning you," Fargo said.

Rosemary giggled mischievously. "Oh my, I'm so scared! What will you do, lover? Beat me within an inch of my life with this oak tree of yours?" She tittered convulsively.

The limits of Skye's patience snapped like a frayed rawhide whip and he rolled on top of her. "You brought this on yourself," he said, and mashed his lips down on top of hers. She squirmed and tried to say something, then changed her mind and parted her lips to allow entry to his tongue.

He swooped both hands to her breasts and squeezed them through the fabric, working them as he would pliant clay, determined to arouse her to orgasm if it was the only way he could get his badly needed rest. His leg slid between hers and stroked up and down, his knee brushing against her mound with each upward sweep.

"That's the spirit!" Rosemary breathed when he tore his mouth from hers and began licking her neck. "I knew you had it in you."

"Screw you," Fargo growled.

"Any time, lover."

With a savage motion he hiked her dress to her hips and slid a hand underneath her lacy underthings to cup her mound of Venus. She quivered, stuck her tongue in his ear, and exhaled with all the vigor of a fire-breathing dragon. A tingle shot down his spine, and to spite her, without further ceremony he plunged a long finger into her moist slit as if stabbing her with a dagger.

"Oh, God!" Rosemary yelped, her back arching.

Had Weatherford and Ogden heard? Fargo wondered, and decided he didn't give a damn. She wanted it—she would get it. And with both barrels, as the expression went.

Rosemary gasped when he squeezed her right breast so hard that it almost hurt. Simultaneously, he plunged his finger all the way to the knuckles into her hot hole, drew it back, and plunged again. She lifted her legs and hooked her heels on his back, cooing in rapturous delight.

His own desire mounting steadily, Fargo used his free hand to uncover her glorious breasts. His mouth clamped on her left nipple and he rolled it with his tongue, then he gave her right nipple the same treatment. She panted and pulled on his hair as if she were trying to take his scalp without the benefit of a knife. Wincing, he parted her nether lips and rammed two fingers into the depths of her womanhood.

"You drive me crazy!" Rosemary whispered, delirious with unbridled passion.

So do you, Fargo wanted to say, and not in the way you think. But his mouth and tongue were too preoccupied to bother with words. He lathered her breasts and the soft underside of her neck, then licked the pale, smooth skin between her breasts. All the while his fingers worked like the piston on a steam engine, stoking her furnace, arousing her to ever greater heights.

"Take your time," Rosemary said languidly, her eyes closed. "I want to savor this."

Fargo's jaw flexed. She did, did she? After having the gall to wake him out of his first sound sleep in days? He yanked his fingers from her throbbing box, unfastened his pants, and touched the tip of his organ to her slit.

"What are you doing?" Rosemary asked, looking into his eyes. "Not yet, dummy."

Grinning wickedly, Skye slammed his pole to the hilt into her wet crack and felt her quiver and arch her back. Her breasts mashed against his chest and he lowered his mouth to take a nipple between his lips.

"No!" Rosemary protested, her eyes closed again.

Ignoring her, he established a driving rhythm, his hips pumping in timed cadence. The exquisite sensation of her silken sheath enclosing his manhood made his throat constrict in anticipation of the ultimate climax.

"No, damn you," Rosemary said, but the actions of her body belied her objections. Her hips pumped as hard as his, rising to meet each thrust with a counterthrust, her legs clamped to his sides and her hands running through his hair in wild abandon. She kissed his throat and gently nibbled on the lobes of both his ears.

Fargo grit his teeth to hold himself in. His organ pulsed, ready to explode. To distract himself he imagined a herd of cattle and began counting them one by one, timing his count to coincide with the strokes of his hips. The longer he waited, the more ecstasy he would experience at the moment of exploding, and the more force he would have behind each thrust. Deep down, he wanted to pound her to pieces.

"Oh!" Rosemary said. "Oh! Oh!"

"Are you ready?" Fargo grunted.

"No! Not yet! I'm not quite there."

"Tough."

Skye Fargo smiled as he dug his knees into the blanket and rammed into Rosemary like a man berserk, throwing his whole weight into the plunge, lifting her fanny off the ground with each rocking motion. Her head snapped back, her lips parted in astonishment, and her eyelids fluttered uncontrollably.

"No!" she whined, thrashing. "No!" And then, pressing her body to his, she clung to him for dear life and moaned. "Oh, yes! Yes! Yes!"

He threw all inhibitions to the wind and tried to drive his organ all the way up into her throat. Their pelvises smacked into each other with the intensity of an Indian drumbeat. Sweat caked his skin.

"I can't stand it!" Rosemary cried, forgetting herself.

Skye smirked.

"Don't stop! Don't ever stop!"

He stopped. Without warning, he abruptly held perfectly still although his organ was doing a magnificent imitation of a volcano about to burst its top.

"What the—?" Rosemary blurted, her eyes locking on his.

"Think I'll catch some sleep now," Fargo told her, barely able to keep his body under control.

"Like hell you will," Rosemary said, and impulsively bit his chin. Then she laughed and gripped his face in both hands. "You beast, you. I guess I had that coming."

Skye grinned. "Ready then?"

"Do me like you've never done anyone, lover."

"Hussy."

"And loving every minute of it. Now shut up and fuck my brains out."

He did. He lunged and stroked and rubbed and caressed until they were both pulsating and gasping, on the very brink. And only then, when she sobbed in his ear and dug her nails into his back, did he give her what she wanted. He came with an intensity that surprised even him, and it seemed as if he would spurt forever. Finally he spent and simply lay on top of her, catching his breath. She hardly moved. When at weary last he slid out of her womanhood and rolled onto his side, she was already asleep.

"Figures," he muttered, and drifted into the fringes of

slumberland. If she woke up later and tried to ply her feminine wiles, he made himself a promise to tie her up until morning. Not that he didn't like making love to her. Quite the opposite. But tomorrow promised to be a day fraught with danger and he needed his rest.

A man had to have a sense of priorities.

# 15

By Skye's estimation they were within two or three miles of the hidden valley when he spied the war party heading south, perhaps more warriors going to join the same band that had attacked the cabin. He was in a draw a quarter of a mile to the west, screened by trees, the others behind him.

"Must be thirty or more," Carl Weatherford commented.

"More than we can handle," Ogden said.

Fargo squinted up at the afternoon sun. They had ridden hard to reach the valley well before nightfall. He didn't want to go into that stygian gap after dark when there might be Paiutes lurking to ambush him. For all he knew, the Indians had found Slade and Lida and were waiting for him to return. It wouldn't have taken much torture for Lida to break down and tell everything she knew. For that matter, few people, including the strongest of men, could hold up under Indian questioning. Being skinned alive or having fingernails wrenched out did a remarkable job of loosening the tongue.

He waited until the war party was well gone and the dust of their passage had settled before he emerged from the draw and continued toward the gap. The Sharps rested across his thighs, his thumb on the hammer. They were in the very heart of Paiute country. At any moment Indians could appear.

"Where did you leave Lida?" Rosemary asked, her concern transparent.

Fargo pointed at the pair of barren hills far ahead. "Between them," he disclosed, "in a cave of sorts. They have plenty of water and I left them some jerky. They should be fine."

"If the Paiutes didn't find them."

He didn't care to aggravate her anxiety by telling her he shared her worry. Alertly scanning the land, he cautiously worked his way ever nearer to the gap. When they were about a mile off, he reined up and pointed at a rocky overhang in the shadows of a nearby ravine. "Wait there until I get back."

"You're not going alone," Rosemary said.

"Yeah," Weatherford threw in. "We won't hear of it."

"I can move quieter by myself," Fargo said. "I'll be in and out before the Paiutes have any idea we're in the area. If all of us go we raise the risk of being discovered. Do you want that to happen?"

None of them did. Their silence said as much.

"Didn't think so. Stay low. Don't let the extra horses stray off. We'll need them for Lida and Slade."

With that Fargo urged the stallion across a flat stretch and into brush beyond. Finding the stream proved easy thanks to the trees growing along both low banks. He moved the pinto into the center of the sluggish water to hide his tracks.

A flock of sparrows flew up from a thicket on his right.

Instantly, Skye brought the pinto to a trot. The startled birds would attract the attention of any Indians nearby and he must get somewhere else fast. A quarter of a mile fell to his rear and nothing happened, leading him to conclude there were no Paiutes in the immediate vicinity. But he refused to relax his vigilance.

When he could distinguish the sheer walls of the gap he slowed and held the Sharps in his left hand. From this side of the twin hills it was apparent there had originally been only one and erosion had worn down the intervening ground until now there were two. He saw no Indians on the slopes, nor any close to the gap.

In order to study the defile before riding in, he stopped under the drooping branches of a young willow. The shade felt refreshing. Straightening to eliminate a kink in his back, he happened to glance down at the soft soil bordering the stream and was glad he did.

Etched as clear as day were two sets of footprints, the heavy boots of a limping man and the lighter tracks of a woman at his side, helping to support him.

What was this? He swung down and crouched to touch the earth that had been pressed down by the weight of

149

the couple. By gauging the firmness of the soil and allowing for the warping and drying effects of the hot days and cool nights, he calculated the time elapsed since Slade and Lida went by. Since the dirt hadn't yet had time to congeal and harden, and since the tracks were only marginally dry, he guessed not more than twenty-four hours and probably less than eighteen had gone by.

Puzzled, he mounted and reversed direction, staying beside the tracks. He was annoyed at himself for not noticing the footprints sooner. Carelessness like that could prove costly at the wrong time and place.

Slade and Lida had followed the stream for over a hundred yards, moving rapidly as indicated by the longer than normal strides each had taken.

He reflected on whether they had been discovered and were being chased. But if so, there would have been Paiute tracks or hoofprints overlapping theirs, and there were none. So the pair must have been fleeing because they feared being discovered. Perhaps they had spotted Paiutes near the east end of the gap and decided to leave rather than risk detection. It was the only reason that made sense.

Suddenly the tracks left the stream and penetrated into a rough and tumble tract of mesquite, rabbit brush, and sage, as well as a few junipers and piñon pines. The undergrowth was a dense wall, impossible for a horse to penetrate.

Not about to leave the Ovaro, Fargo rode west seeking a game trail or other path that would take him north. If Rafe and Lida were hiding in there, they might see him and come out. Shortly, he located a grassy strip extending from the stream far into the brush, and he turned to the right. The thickets hemmed him in, cutting him off from the outside world. He heard insects buzzing, the plod of the Ovaro's hoofs, and the creak of his saddle. Once a bee buzzed by his face.

Sweat trickled down his brow and along his spine. He wished he could find a cold mountain lake and take a dip. In the sky a solitary cloud shaped much like a Conestoga sailed eastward on billowy white wheels. To the northeast, well past the hills, rose five thin columns of smoke from fires in the Paiute village. Right about now the women would be starting to prepare the evening meals, and the thought of a savory venison stew made his mouth water. Or perhaps one was roasting a haunch of bighorn sheep.

Skye caught himself and shook his head. What the hell was he trying to do? Get killed? He mustn't allow his mind to wander again. He leaned down and examined the ground, seeking more footprints. The ground was harder, the grass a carpet, neither conducive to leaving tracks. Other than old deer tracks the soil was a blank page.

He came to where the strip of grass narrowed and ended, preventing him from going any further mounted. Turning the Ovaro sideways, he stood in the stirrups and surveyed the vegetation, strongly tempted to give a shout. He saw a fly and a small white butterfly, nothing larger. Slade and Lida had done a damn fine job of losing themselves in the brush.

About to lift the reins, he tensed as a crackling noise issued from under mesquite off to the northeast. A furtive figure glided from cover to cover, a figure wearing a dress.

"Lida?"

She stood, her face lit with joy, her hands clasped to her bosom. Dirt smudged her cheeks, her hair had lost its coiffured glory, and her dress bore quite a few tears. "Skye! Thank goodness it's you!"

"Where's Slade?"

Lida nodded at the mesquite. "Sleeping. His fever has gone down but he's still bad off. I didn't want to wake him when I thought I heard a horse coming." Tears trickled down her dirty cheeks. "I was so afraid it was Paiutes."

"Did they find you in the gap?"

"No, but we saw several watering their horses at the east end. Rafe figured it would be wiser for us to light out."

"Smart man. Need some help with him?"

"No, thank you. He's too proud. He insists on doing everything himself," Lida said, pride in her tone. "I'll fetch him." She began to depart, then paused. "Oh, dear. I forgot. What about Rosemary and Howard?"

"Rosemary is safe and waiting. Howard is maggot food."

"Rafe will be disappointed. He's been looking forward to blowing Pete's brains out."

Skye watched her race off. Now all he had to do was get the pair of them to the horses and ride like hell for California. And hope no more war parties showed their painted hides. He cradled the Sharps in his left arm, waiting impatiently.

Rafe Slade was a shadow of his former self. He was as pale as a sheet, his features gaunt. He favored his left leg, wincing with every stride. Only the fierce gleam of determination in his eyes showed that deep within still burned the fiery temperament that had made him a curly wolf among less civilized men. "About to give you up for lost," he said gruffly.

"You're not the only one too ornery to die."

"We could sure use some grub," Slade said. "I can't get enough to eat. Must be my wound. We finished off the jerky yesterday about noon and later I clubbed a lizard to death."

Lida's nose crinkled. "Never thought I'd eat raw lizard. My stomach does flip-flops when I think about it."

"You should have seen her," Slade said with a grin. "She kept her eyes closed the whole time and pinched her nose shut so she couldn't smell the meat." He placed a hand on her shoulder. "She did fine. Real fine."

Skye climbed down. If he should live to be a hundred and ten, he doubted he would ever understand how the human heart worked. Under ordinary circumstances, the prospect of a woman in Lida's profession falling for an outlaw like Rafe Slade was as slim as a rail. Yet out here, thrown together by circumstance, their lives in jeopardy, forced to get along in order to survive, they had discarded all of their usual airs and prejudices and related honestly and openly. And look at the result. "Get on board," he said.

"I can walk," Rafe said.

"We have over a mile to go. Do you want that wound to begin bleeding again?"

"Do like the man says," Lida chided.

Slade reluctantly mounted, with help, and Fargo took the reins to lead the Ovaro. He didn't want the pinto to act up, which it was inclined to do if a stranger forked its back. The Sharps in his right hand, he retraced his

152

path to the stream and stopped to double-check before stepping into the open.

"Lida told me Pete is dead," Slade whispered.

Fargo nodded. "Paiutes."

"Was it quick?"

Again Fargo nodded.

"Too bad. The bastard deserved to be skinned alive and staked out on a red ant hill."

They moved into the middle of the water and headed westward. Skye paused frequently to look and listen. In hostile Indian territory a good pair of eyes and ears often did more to preserve a traveler's scalp than either a gun or a knife, and he wanted to avoid another fight with the Paiutes at all costs.

Their progress was uneventful, at first. Skye came to where he had to leave the stream and made for the ravine where the others would be waiting. He held to the low ground and, whenever possible, took advantage of the brush to conceal their movements. When he spied the ravine he smiled. Soon they would all be riding toward California and in a few days the Paiute war would be no more than vivid memories.

"Skye?" Lida said.

He glanced at her, she pointed to the rear, and anger flared as he beheld a sizable group of horsemen on one of the hills above the gap. There were a dozen or better warriors in all and they appeared to be gazing directly at him.

"Have they seen us?" Lida asked in horror.

The band, with much waving of arms and weapons, rode down the slope to the base of the hill.

"They've seen us," Slade said.

"Move it," Fargo directed, breaking into a run and pulling on the reins. The Paiutes would need five minutes or better to overtake them and by then they should be at the ravine. But from there on it would be nip and tuck, and with Slade in the condition he was in outrunning the braves would be extremely difficult if not impossible. Grimly, he sprinted for the rocky overhang. When over a hundred yards remained, he saw Rosemary, Weatherford, and Ogden break from cover leading the spare mounts. He stopped and assisted Slade in sliding from the saddle.

"Lida!" Rosemary cried in delight, leaping off her horse before the animal had completely stopped to warmly embrace her friend.

"It's so wonderful to see you again," Lida said, the tears flowing once more.

Carl Weatherford was staring at Rafe. "You might as well hear it now. The boys and me stood up to Pete Howard and made him back down. We'd decided we didn't want anything to do with a woman-killer. If you harbor any hard feelings, air them now and we'll get it over with."

"There are no hard feelings," Slade said. "Any loyalty I had to Pete died when he cut out on us and left us for the Paiutes."

Weatherford sighed in relief. "Good to hear it. I dreaded the notion of tangling with you."

Fargo cleared his throat. "If we don't do some hard riding we'll all be up to our necks in Paiutes before you know it," he said, and added for the benefit of Rosemary and the miners, "A band spotted us. They can't be more than a minute or two away."

"Then what are we waiting for?" Weatherford responded. "Let's get the hell out of here."

As usual Skye took the lead. He rode southwest, intending eventually to intercept the rutted route used by the Pony Express and the stage line. There were several hours of daylight remaining. If they could keep the Paiutes at bay until dark, they stood an excellent chance of escaping.

A gully beckoned on the right and into it he went, keeping the pinto to a canter. For half a mile he followed a winding course, until there was ample vegetation on both rims, and then he went up and over the side. A plain led up to a low mountain range. He turned south, the mountains on his flank until a wide canyon appeared. Hoping there would be an outlet, he rode deep into the canyon until a deer trail offered a means of ascending to the top.

Here he stopped to study the panoramic sweep of countryside they had traversed. Inexplicably, no dust clouds were to be seen. Mystified, he pressed on. Every second of daylight that passed without incident brought nightfall and safety that much nearer.

A long plain of mesquite and brush brought them to a salty mud flat they skirted to the west only to encounter an extensive white alkali flat. Nothing grew, not so much as a single blade of grass. Waves of heat shimmered and danced, and they were the only moving creatures on the vast white expanse. The soaring temperature made them slow down. And they left tracks a child could follow.

Over an hour later they came to the edge of the flat and the welcome sight of heavy brush extending for many miles. They urged their mounts to increased speed to make up the time lost crossing the flat.

"Do you see what I see?" Rafe Slade asked, nodding to the northeast.

A single column of smoke rose as straight as a pillar.

"The damn Paiutes," Weatherford said.

Ogden cursed a blue streak, then concluded with, "Must be two miles off."

"What are they saying?" Lida inquired.

Fargo could answer that. "They know where we are and they're signaling to tell any war parties who happen to be in this region to cut us off."

"Not again," Rosemary said.

Their horses badly needed rest. Everyone was aware of it. But they goaded the tired animals ever onward, knowing to stop now invited disaster. Some of the Indian ponies started to misbehave, to jerk at their reins and balk. The Ovaro exhibited the best endurance, maintaining the pace the other horses were forced to match.

Yet another of the more than thirty mountain ranges marking the upland area through which they were fleeing now appeared before them. This range, like most in the territory, extended from north to south. An arm, however, extended due east for several miles. The formation created an enormous natural L.

Fargo didn't like it at all. Their course would bring them to the junction of the main chain and the offshoot, and there might not be a way over the top. They would be hemmed in on two sides, a perfect time for the Paiutes to strike. He was about to swing to the east when Carl Weatherford spoke up.

"Hey, I know where we are. There's a pass up yonder that will bring us down close to the stage line."

"You've been through it?"

"No, but I talked to a couple of prospectors who used it pretty regular when they were prospecting up in this neck of the woods."

Skye gazed at the ragged peaks, assessing the odds. If they could cross the range well ahead of any pursuit, they should be able to reach Tahoe without any more trouble. The climb looked steep and their mounts were already flagging, but the gain outweighed the risk. So he took the bottom slope at a trot but was moving at a walk by the time the stallion had climbed a hundred feet.

"I swear I'll never leave civilization again," Rosemary commented, riding on his left. "When we reach San Francisco I'm going to dig in roots and stay put for the rest of my life."

"Fixing to get hitched?" Ogden asked.

"Hell, no. I'm not ready to be put out to pasture yet. But a house of my own would be nice, maybe with a little garden where I could tend flowers," Rosemary said wistfully.

"You'll be welcome at our house any time," Lida said.

Rosemary glanced at her. "*Our* house?"

"Didn't I mention that Rafe and I are going to be married the first chance we have?" Lida replied, smiling demurely. "He proposed while we were waiting for Skye and you to return."

"My, my. You must have had an interesting time back there," Rosemary joked.

"Talking about marriage is fine," Carl Weatherford said, "but I wouldn't get ahead of myself if I was you." He lifted an arm to the northeast.

Skye didn't want to look. He knew what he would see. His stomach muscles tightening, he shifted his gaze and beheld a war party not all that far off. The warriors had stayed in the brush to conceal their presence until the right moment.

"They'll catch us," Ogden said. "We'll never reach the pass before them."

"Yes, we will," Fargo stated, wishing he were as confident as he sounded. Had he been alone he might well do it because the Ovaro was in good shape. But he wasn't about to desert the others; he must stay with them no matter how slowly they climbed. Out came the Sharps and he fed a cartridge into the rifle. "I'll slow them down," he offered, drawing rein. "The rest of you keep riding."

"We won't leave you," Rosemary objected.

"Do it," Fargo commanded. "I'll be along shortly."

Weatherford motioned for Rosemary to continue the ascent and she did, frowning all the while.

Turning the Ovaro downhill, Fargo sat with the Sharps in his lap and tried to estimate the number of approaching braves. He counted to fifteen and had to stop because the dust obscured the rest of them. It might very well be the same band he had observed riding to the south from the valley. Not that it mattered. There were more than enough warriors to deal with his little party.

The foremost braves drew within range. Skye lifted the Sharps and adjusted the sight, taking his time, not wanting to waste a single shot. If he killed a leader or two the band might have second thoughts. Then again, they might become so enraged they would chase him to the ends of the earth.

He fixed the front sight on the muscular warrior at the head of the war party, aligned the rear sight accordingly, and cocked the weapon. His finger curled around the trigger ever so gently, he held his breath, and squeezed. Out on the plain the warrior threw his arms aloft as if appealing to the Great Spirit, dropped his bow, and pitched headlong to the dirt.

The band never broke their collective stride.

So much for that brilliant idea, Fargo reflected, and reloaded. This time he aimed quickly and fired at the very instant the Sharps leveled. A second brave fell.

Still the band swept closer.

Skye's fingers flew as he reloaded once more. He heard the bark of a gun and saw the puff of smoke from a rifle. The Paiute who fired was a lousy marksman and the shot fell short by a dozen yards, whining off a rock. "See how you like your own medicine," Skye said to himself, and fixed a bead on the rifleman. His shot rolled off across the mountain, and the warrior toppled still clutching his rifle.

Two more guns opened up.

Putting his heels to the stallion, Fargo started toward the pass. He fed in a fresh cartridge, guiding the Ovaro with his legs alone. Behind him the Paiutes were almost to the bottom of the slope. They were in rifle range but fortunately few possessed guns and those who did seldom got to practice due to a chronic shortage of ammunition.

Hundreds of yards higher rode the women, the miners, and Slade. They were well shy of the shadow-shrouded opening that must be the pass.

Skye rapidly climbed sixty or seventy feet, then halted. The warriors were fanning out across the barren bottom slope to prevent him from sweeping around on either side to escape. He had no intention of doing so but they didn't know that. Instead, he aimed at a stocky brave and fired.

As if clubbed in the face, the Paiute hurtled off the rump of his steed and crashed onto the unyielding ground.

Four down, Fargo tallied, but the warriors were coming on strong, whooping and shrieking in typical Indian fashion, a ploy designed to inspire fear in their enemies and courage in their own hearts. Their painted war horses, accustomed to such rugged land, climbed with remarkable agility. He rode higher, reloading as he did. If only he could hold them off until his friends reached the pass!

An arrow swooped out of the sky, then another and another. None scored, but all came uncomfortably close to the pinto. A rifle belched lead and smoke and a bullet ricocheted off a boulder.

Fargo had to put more distance between himself and the war party. He gripped the reins and goaded the pinto up. The steep slope combined with the pull of gravity compelled the Ovaro to struggle with every step. And the higher they went, the steeper it became. He leaned forward to distribute his weight in the saddle more evenly. "Come on," he prompted. "You can do it."

The minutes stretched into eternity. He sweated buckets of perspiration, dampening his buckskins. The saddle became slick. Every so often an arrow buzzed past or thudded into the soil near the Ovaro. The Paiutes were skilled archers, but shooting uphill as they were and while mounted to boot, they couldn't quite get the range.

He didn't stop to fire again since a stationary target would make it easier for them.

"Skye! Up here!"

The anxious cry came from directly above and he tilted his head in surprise to see the pass twenty-five feet off. Rosemary stood in the shelter of a huge boulder, her fists clenched in her worry for his safety. Beside her were Weatherford and Ogden, both holding their rifles.

"You thinned those Injuns out fine," Ogden said as Skye joined them.

"They're still climbing though."

And they were. If nothing else, the Paiutes were as tenacious as bulldogs. A poor tribe they might be, and maybe they didn't have a reputation for being superb fighters as did the Sioux, the Cheyennes, the Apaches, the Comanches, and others. But no one could ever rightfully label the Paiutes as spineless digger Indians, as many had done before the outbreak of hostilities. Never again would the whites take the Paiute tribe lightly.

"They've been spreading out farther and farther," Weatherford said. "I reckon they'll try to outflank us before too long."

Skye brought the Ovaro to a stop next to the rest of the horses and climbed down. The narrow pass was littered with large boulders and slabs of rock that would afford ideal positions from which to fire at the Indians. On both sides reared jagged peaks, and on neither was there so much as a game trail the Paiutes could use to get around them. The way he saw it, ages ago both peaks had been connected by a rim of rock that had collapsed to form the pass. Hefting the Sharps, he ran to the far end thirty yards away. Below stretched a gradual series of slopes and switchbacks terminating in a wide plain. Even from that height the ruts gouged into the earth by the many stages and wagons that had passed en route to California or points east were visible. He pivoted and returned.

Rafe Slade sat propped against a slab. The ride had set his wound to bleeding again. He was paler than before and seemed inordinately weak. Lida was at his side, applying the water from a canteen sparingly to a white cloth and dampening his feverish brow.

Fargo saw Rosemary walk over to them and he stepped

to the north end where the miners were observing the climbing Paiutes. Many of the braves had dismounted and left their horses behind, preferring to dart from cover to cover, using boulders and whatever else offered concealment.

Carl Weatherford glanced at the women and Slade, then turned to Skye and spoke softly so he wouldn't be overheard. "Ogden and I have been doing some talking. There must be thirty or more Injuns closing in on us. We can't hold them off forever. For one thing, we don't have that much ammunition. Sooner or later they'll break into the pass and it will be all over."

"So we got to thinking," Ogden said when his friend paused. "A few of us might be able to keep the redskins pinned down while the rest hightail it for Virginia City or Carson City."

"Might work," Fargo agreed, finding more and more to respect in these men as time went on. Miners, in general, were a rugged, boisterous, and occasionally lawless lot, but they were the salt of the earth in a crisis.

"The three of us could hold the fort while the ladies and Rafe ride out," Weatherford proposed.

"Better get them going," Odgen said, nodding at the slope where most of the Indians were now hidden. "Those devils will be coming for our hair soon."

"I could try and hold the pass alone," Fargo offered.

"You wouldn't last two minutes," Weatherford said. "No insult meant, friend, but no one is that good, not even you."

"Look!" Ogden said, pointing.

All of the warriors were now on foot and inexorably working their way higher. They flitted from boulder to boulder and bush to bush like dust-caked ghosts, their moccasin-clad feet treading silently.

Fargo hastened to the women and Slade. "Mount up," he instructed them. "You're all getting out of here right now."

"What about you?" Rosemary asked.

"I'll be along in a while," Skye said, taking her elbow. "Once you're at the bottom head west. Eventually you'll find an Express station that is still in business or else you'll reach Carson City." He steered her toward the horses.

"But—"

"Don't argue, dammit. Now is not the time."

She looked at him, about to protest, then at Lida and Slade as Rafe stood with Lida's aid.

"They'll need you," Fargo said.

Rosemary bit her lower lip, her face a study in indecision. "I wish there was another way."

"There isn't," Fargo said, and swept her onto her horse before she could resist. Avoiding her gaze, he assisted Slade in mounting, then stepped back.

"Sorry, Fargo," Rafe said weakly.

Skye nodded.

"We'll be expecting you to catch up soon," Lida said cheerfully. "When we get to Carson City the drinks will be on us."

"You're on," Fargo declared. He saw Rosemary move as if to climb down, and with a quick stride he whipped off his hat and struck her mount on the rump. The horse took off for the opposite end of the pass, trailed by Lida and Rafe Slade. He lingered and waved when Rosemary twisted and lifted her hand. Then he spun on his heels and stalked to the edge of the upper slope. There wasn't a Paiute anywhere.

"I figure we have less than an hour before the sun sets," Weatherford said. "If we can keep the bucks pinned down until then, we can cut out."

Skye was examining the pass with a view to their defense. "Ogden, take our horses to the far end and tie them there. We don't want them hit by a stray bullet or arrow, and we don't want them running off once the fight starts."

"Will do," the miner said, and broke into a run.

"Where do you want me?" Weatherford inquired.

"Pick any spot you like," Fargo said, moving behind a slab near the edge that would partially protect him. From where he crouched he could see the entire side of the mountain. Far, far off, toward the village in the valley, rose a smoke signal too faint to read.

Weatherford squatted in the shadow of a boulder. "If anything happens to me," he remarked, "would you get word to Mario Ronca at the Aces Saloon in Virginia City? He's an old friend of mine and he'll know who to contact."

"Mario Ronca," Fargo repeated. "Aces Saloon."

"I'm obliged."

A Paiute brave abruptly appeared on the slope not ten feet off, his sturdy legs pumping as he raced for the pass, an arrow nocked to the string on his bow.

Fargo snapped off a shot that cored the brave's brain, and as if on signal all hell broke loose. Paiutes rained lead and arrows on the mouth of the pass while slipping ever closer. He reloaded the Sharps, spied a warrior snaking up on his right, and sent a bullet into the man's body.

Weatherford opened up, firing as rapidly as targets materialized and then dropping down to keep from becoming just another casualty of the fierce war.

A warrior holding a hatchet dashed from concealment not six feet from the boulder sheltering Weatherford.

Having a clean shot, Fargo nailed the Paiute smack in the sternum. The warrior did a graceful pirouette, then toppled.

Braves began popping up right and left, rising long enough to unleash arrows or fire rifles and ducking from sight again. In their haste they usually missed, but the tactic had the effect of keeping Skye and Weatherford pinned down when they should be picking off warriors to stop the Paiutes from gaining the pass.

Fargo heard footsteps and Ogden took up a post behind a boulder on his right.

"Let's give these heathens hell!"

The converging warriors intensified their fire. Arrows whizzed from all directions. Bullets smacked into slabs and screeched off of rocks.

Something tugged at Fargo's hat but he ignored it. He was too busy loading and shooting and loading and shooting to pay attention to much else. His companions were working their rifles like madmen, too, and among the three of them they were temporarily keeping the Paiutes at bay. He saw a warrior fall and lie still and another take a slug in the arm, stagger, then vanish. Gun smoke drifted into the pass and stung his nostrils when he inhaled.

Thwarted and frustrated, the Paiutes rose en masse and charged. Guns boomed, arrows and lances whistled through the air. Two of the warriors dropped. Seconds later so did two more. The foremost braves were almost to the crest when the force of their charge was broken by the effective marksmanship of the three defenders. The Paiutes retreated, disappearing as if swallowed by the soil.

"We did it!" Ogden cried. "We gave 'em what for!"

Fitting a new cartridge into the Sharps, Fargo threw some verbal water on the miner's burning enthusiasm. "They'll try again."

"Let the butchers come. I'm ready," Ogden stated, and cackled triumphantly.

"How many did we kill?" Weatherford wondered.

"There's no way of telling," Fargo said, counting four corpses scattered on the slope. The Paiutes had probably dragged others off and would do the same with those four as soon as dark descended. Which reminded him. Shifting, he squinted at the setting sun. Forty minutes or so of daylight were left.

"Slade and the ladies will be halfway to the bottom by now," Weatherford remarked.

"They'll make it," Ogden predicted. "We'll make damn certain they do."

No one said a word after that. Fargo leaned a shoulder on the slab and mopped his forehead and neck with his sleeve. The Paiutes were bound to realize they must take the pass by nightfall or their quarry would escape, so he could expect another full-scale attack at any moment. With the Sharps loaded and cocked, he scanned the slope. Partway down, near a bush, was a light patch of brown. He noted the outline of the object and smirked. It was a foot. Some folks, Indians and whites, were born careless. Resting the barrel against the slab, he aimed at the center of the brown patch and fired. The Sharps cracked and a lean form leaped erect like a stricken deer, then fell from sight.

"Got him in the foot!" Ogden said, laughing.

Fargo removed the spent cartridge while somberly anticipating the next onslaught. He expected the Paiutes to swarm from concealment all at once and rely on their overwhelming numbers to carry them up and into the pass. Bending down, he loosened the Arkansas toothpick in its slender leather sheath in his boot in case the fighting became man-to-man.

The blazing sun sank lower and lower. In the narrow pass the shadows lengthened and darkened.

What the hell were the Paiutes waiting for? Fargo reflected irritably, and then in a rush of insight saw the reason. The twin peaks prevented the fading sunlight from touching the north slope. In another minute the upper portion of the slope would be enveloped in shadow, enabling the warriors to creep even closer before opening fire. "Get set," he warned the miners. "Any second now."

"Maybe they've had enough," Ogden said. "Maybe they're not as tough as we think."

"I wouldn't count on it."

A piercing war whoop shattered the stillness and the very earth seemed to disgorge frenzied braves who sped toward the summit on winged feet. Bowstrings quivered and rifles barked. Three of them gained the pass.

Fargo fired at the same time the miners did, their shots blending into a blast of thunder that knocked the three braves from the rim. His hands were a blur as he reloaded and fired again. And again and again. He lost count of the number of times. Vaguely, he was aware of Weatherford and Ogden firing like men possessed.

The Paiutes refused to buckle. For every warrior downed another was instantly ready to take his place. Arrows and bullets flew as thick as bees in a swarm.

In the midst of the battle the loud grunt was barely audible but Fargo heard it and glanced to his right to see Ogden with a lance through the chest. The miner was on his knees, futilely grasping the shaft. His hands slipped off and he looked at Skye, then grinned at some private joke and smacked onto his face in the dirt.

Carl Weatherford was still shooting.

Darkness shrouded the pass. Dead braves lay sprawled in the mouth. Others were desperately trying to scramble over the bodies to get at the whites while still others tried to keep the whites pinned down. Four finally attained the summit simultaneously.

Fargo's right hand swooped to the Colt and he got off his first shot as one of the braves drew back a bowstring. He downed a second enemy, saw the third let an arrow fly and killed him with a slug to the brain. The fourth brave dodged behind a boulder as a fifth and sixth appeared at the rim. "We can't hold them!" he shouted to Weatherford. "Fall back!"

Heeding his own advice, he backpedaled swiftly, firing yet again to discourage the Paiutes from pressing him too hard. He glanced at Weatherford's hiding place, about to urge the man to get his butt moving, when he discovered the miner would never be moving again. An arrow had caught Weatherford at the base of the throat.

Paiutes were pouring into the pass.

All that could be done had been done. Skye Fargo whirled and ran for his life, threading among the boulders and slabs, with over a dozen shrieking fiends on his heels. He barely got into the saddle before the leaders of the pack appeared and he fired, slowing them, then he yanked on the reins and galloped out of the pass and down the slope. An arrow missed his right shoulder by the width of the fringe on his buckskins. A bullet took a piece out of his hat. The sun had set, and into the gathering black of night he rode, his features chiseled in granite. Behind him the pass echoed to savage yells.

He rode up to the Pony Express station located at the foot of Lake Tahoe as the sun crested the eastern horizon and the new day came alive with the chirping of birds and the nickering of Express stock eager to be fed.

The door opened and out stepped a beefy man in a flannel shirt and trousers. He took a pace, then saw the big man astride the pinto stallion and drew up short in surprise. Both horse and rider were exhausted, caked with dust and grime. Neither seemed capable of going another yard. "Howdy," he said tentatively. "The name is Berry. I run this station."

Without saying a word the big man lifted the *mochila* from behind his saddle and rode up to Berry. "This belongs to your company," he said, and let go.

Bewildered, Berry stared at the *mochila*, then at the rider. No one other than Express personnel were supposed to touch the mail pouches, and he opened his mouth to interrogate the stranger. Something stopped him. He saw a look in the big man's eyes that sent a shiver down his spine.

*"Adiós,"* the stranger said, wheeling the tired stallion.

"Wait!" Berry blurted, but the rider paid no attention.

He watched the man ride off, at a loss to know what to do. Cupping a hand to his mouth, he yelled the first thing that came into his head. "Thanks, mister. Appreciate your returning company property. Hope it wasn't too much trouble."

The big man kept going and was soon lost in the morning haze.

## LOOKING FORWARD!

**The following is the opening
section from the next novel in the exciting
*Trailsman* series from Signet:**

## THE TRAILSMAN #128
## SNAKE RIVER BUTCHER

*1859, the Snake River region,
where those who traveled the Oregon Trail
did so at their own risk . . .*

The big man astride the splendid pinto stallion reined
up abruptly as he topped a rise and saw the five men
camped below on the bank of the Snake River. A thin
column of smoke wafted skyward from their camp fire,
and the breeze carried the delicious aroma of brewing
coffee to his sensitive nostrils. His stomach growled, re-
minding him that he had not had a decent cup of coffee
in days. Although he had rationed his supply, he had run
out on the long trail from Denver to the remote, rugged
Snake River country.

Ordinarily Skye Fargo kept to himself. But he was new
to the area and had heard rumors of Indian trouble. It
might be wise to learn what he could before he ventured
further on his quest, and with that in mind he touched
his spurs to the Ovaro's muscular flanks and rode directly
toward the camp.

One of the men spotted him right away and said something to the rest that brought all of them to their feet,
rifles in hand. They were a grubby lot, wearing soiled
flannel shirts, faded, patched trousers, and hats that had
seen better days ages ago.

As Skye neared the camp his every instinct told him he had made a mistake. He saw expressions of blatant envy on the faces of several of the bunch as they admired his stallion and his gear, and he noticed the tallest of the lot whisper to the others and immediately a burly character started to edge off to the right while another man did likewise on the left. They were so obvious he almost laughed. Instead he rested his right hand on his thigh within inches of his Colt.

"Howdy, stranger," the tall one greeted him with a generous smile that revealed several of his front teeth were missing.

Fargo drew rein ten feet away and simply nodded. He stared at the speaker but kept track of the pair trying not so cleverly to outflank him.

"Light and sit a while," the tall man said, motioning at the battered coffeepot beside the crackling flames. "We have plenty of coffee if you're thirsty."

"Another time," Fargo said pleasantly, letting them think they had him duped so they would be all the more shocked when he demonstrated otherwise.

The tall one advanced a stride, the barrel of his rifle slowly inching higher. "What can we do for you then?"

"Back in Denver there was talk of Indian trouble in this neck of the woods. Have you had any problem?"

"Us?" the tall one said, and most of them snickered as if at a joke. "Can't say as we have. There were some Mormons east of here a ways who got run off a while back. A few were killed and scalped, as I recollect." He smirked. "But they were just no-account Mormons."

"Too bad it wasn't you and your outfit," Fargo said.

The tall man blinked, perhaps not believing he had heard correctly, and then he realized he had and began to elevate the rifle, his finger sliding over the trigger.

Skye Fargo was in no mood to go easy on the cutthroats. He had been riding hard for more days than he cared to remember and he was tired and sore and hungry. His right hand was a blur as the Colt flashed up and out, and his first shot tore into the tall man's throat. His second shot, so closely spaced the twin blasts were one sound, ripped into the man's chest and staggered him. The tall man let go of his rifle, spun, and toppled.

Fargo was already in motion, twisting to send a slug into the forehead of the skinny sidewinder on the right who was trying to bring his rifle to bear. Then he shifted again, covering the remaining three, all of whom froze as if abruptly encased in ice. "Any more of you anxious to meet your Maker?" he asked calmly, and cocked the Colt to accent his meaning.

"Don't shoot, mister!" blurted a man sporting a walrus mustache. He tossed his rifle to the ground. "Please don't shoot!"

The other two followed his example and in moments all three were clawing for the clouds without having been ordered to do so.

"I was hoping you'd make a fight of it," Fargo said and gestured with the Colt to indicate they should back up past the fire. "Unload your hardware," he directed, and once they had gingerly discarded their pistols he swung down, being careful to keep his six-shooter on them the whole time, then stepped to the fire. "This coffee sure does smell good," he commented, bending to lift the pot. The bottom was hot but the top rim only warm. He tilted the narrow spout and took a sip, then smacked his lips. "Who made this?"

Walrus pointed at the tall man, lying prone in a spreading puddle of blood. "Harry did."

"He wasn't much of a robber, but he had a knack for making a fine brew," Skye quipped and swallowed some more.

"What do you aim to do with us?" Walrus inquired nervously.

"I should shoot you."

"No!" exclaimed the bearded man on the left. "I have a wife and kids. You can't!"

Slowly, deliberately, Fargo pointed the Colt at him and the man took a step to the rear, his lips quivering in abject fear, his legs trembling as if he had to take a leak and was desperately holding it in.

"Please!" he whined. "We never meant to harm you."

Fargo shot him. The revolver boomed and bucked in

his hand, and the man reacted in the same way as would someone slammed by a sledgehammer, by flying a good three feet to crash down on his back. His features hard as granite, Fargo took a few steps forward. The other two were imitating trees.

"Oh, God!" the man on the ground wailed, clutching the neat hole in his right shoulder and writhing in torment. "You plugged me! You plugged me!"

"I can do it again if you don't shut up."

The man fell silent, gritting his teeth.

"I can't abide liars," Fargo stated gruffly. "Particularly when they were fixing to kill me and steal everything I own."

"We weren't—" the wounded man protested, then caught himself and clamped his thin lips shut.

"That's better," Fargo said, moving back around the fire. He squatted and sipped more of the refreshing coffee, his gaze roving over their shabby clothes and to their horses tethered nearby. "Strange," he said.

Walrus took the bait. "What is, mister?"

"All of you could pass for walking rags but you all own horses as fine as any I've ever seen," Fargo noted. "Why is that?"

"A good horse out in these parts can mean the difference between living and dying," Walrus replied. "You know that." He paused. "We'd rather spend our money on a fine horse any day than on new Levi's. Pants and such can't outrun Injuns."

The shifty bastard had a point, but Fargo didn't believe him for a second. Still, he couldn't prove anything and despite what these men might believe, he wasn't a coldhearted murderer. "Were I you I would make myself scarce in this territory," he informed them. "I'll probably be wandering around for a while, and if I ever lay eyes on any of you again you'd better be able to slap leather faster than me."

"None of us are that fast," said the robber who had not uttered a word until now.

"Should help you decide what to do," Fargo said, rising so he could arch his back and stretch. "How far is it to Fort Hall?"

"About fifteen miles," Walrus answered.

Fargo glanced at the gurgling river, estimating the depth. "I'd be willing to bet none of you gents have bothered to take a bath this year, have you?"

They exchanged worried looks.

"So?" Walrus answered.

"So I figure it's time for all of you to take one," Fargo said and nodded at the waterway that some claimed flowed over a thousand miles, all the way from the Continental Divide in the northern Rockies to where it merged into the mighty Columbia River a few hundred miles shy of the Pacific Ocean. "Jump in."

"You're loco!" Walrus declared.

Fargo grinned and wagged the Colt. "Some folks might agree with you. But I figure I'm doing the next whore you sleep with a favor by sparing her nose some misery. So don't be shy. Jump right in, clothes and all."

None of them moved. The robber on the ground groaned loudly, his hand pressed tight over the bullet hole.

"I'm waiting," Fargo said.

Walrus shook his head. "No way, stranger. I'll be damned if I will."

"You'll be dead if you don't."

Scowling in disgust, the third man moved to the edge of the low bank and contemplated the shallow water flowing sluggishly past. He bent down to dip a hand in the cold water and shivered. "I'll freeze my ass off."

"It's better than lead poisoning," Fargo pointed out, enjoying himself immensely. These men had asked for trouble by stupidly trying to rob him and he intended to give them an object lesson they wouldn't soon forget. He suspected the gang had a string of robberies and perhaps killings to their credit. They probably deserved to be the guests of honor at a necktie party, but he wasn't a vigilante. He watched the wounded man stand, and together the trio stepped tentatively into the Snake. When the water swirled past their ankles they halted. "Keep on going," he directed.

Exhibiting as much enthusiasm as they would if they were being forced to wrestle a grizzly, the three robbers walked out farther. The water level rose to their knees and again they stopped.

"Not yet," Fargo told them and cracked a grin. The ploy served a twofold purpose. Not only did it humiliate them, but it would leave them in no position to try and shoot him in the back when he departed. He moved to where their discarded revolvers lay and began picking them up.

"What the hell are you doing now?" demanded the man with the mustache.

"You can't leave us defenseless!" cried the wounded one.

"I'm tempted," Fargo responded. "But even sons of bitches like you deserve a chance to protect themselves." He walked over to a dense thicket and proceeded to toss the revolvers one at a time into the heaviest tangle of growth.

"We'll remember you for this, mister," Walrus said.

"I'm shaking in my boots," Fargo said and gathered their rifles into his arms. He strolled to the river, deposited his burden at his feet, then gripped one of the weapons by the barrel and hefted it.

"No!" Walrus shouted.

Ignoring him, Fargo swept his arm to one side, then whipped the rifle forward and released his grip. Sunlight glinted off the metal as the rifle sailed end over end and splashed down a dozen yards up river from the would-be robbers. One by one he tossed each rifle as far as he could, and when the last of the long guns lay at the bottom of the Snake, he turned his attention to his crestfallen enemies who were standing in waist-deep water. "Keep on going," he instructed them.

If looks could kill they would have shriveled him like a withering plant.

When the Snake rose to just under their arms Fargo twirled his Colt into its holster and beamed. "That should do, boys. Thanks for the entertainment." Pivoting, he went to their horses and commenced untying every animal.

"You have a name, bastard?" Walrus called out. "I want to know who to ask for."

"The handle is Skye Fargo," he informed them and heard the excited muttering that ensued. Given the tales told about him around many a campfire and in many a saloon from the Mississippi to California, he wouldn't be at all surprised if they had heard of him. Not that it mattered in the least. He paid no attention to his notoriety. His main concern during all his widespread traveling was simply staying alive.

He removed his hat and slapped it on the rump of the nearest horse. "Heeyaahhh!" he bellowed, then waved the hat wildly and jumped up and down several times. The horses wheeled and raced westward, raising a small cloud of dust in their wake, and were soon lost to view in a tract of woodland.

Feeling quite pleased with himself, Fargo walked to the Ovaro and mounted. The three men were glaring sullenly. He added insult to injury by giving a cheery wave and resumed his journey, heading in the general direction he expected to find Fort Hall. Several times he glanced back. When he had gone over a hundred yards the three men waded to shore and clambered out of the river. The one with the walrus mustache shook a fist and shouted obscenities, then all three hurried to the thicket where their six-shooters had been tossed.

Fargo wasn't worried. The range was too great for an accurate pistol shot, and those three had impressed him as being unable to hit the broad side of a steamboat with a paddle. Soon he came to the woodland and angled to the northwest. There had been few trees the last twenty miles or better and he was grateful for the shade. A last look showed one of the robbers venturing into the Snake in an attempt to retrieve the rifles.

He put the trio from his mind as of no further importance and pressed on. There was an hour or so of daylight left and he wanted to take full advantage of the time to get as close to Fort Hall as he could before night set in. He'd decided earlier to hold off entering the fort until the next morning. A good night's sleep would refresh him for the job ahead.

The Snake River area abounded with wildlife. There were birds everywhere—sparrows flitting about, a few gorgeous tanagers perched on the highest branches, nutcrackers seeking food, and an occasional woodpecker or two. Daredevil squirrels leaped from tree to tree while chipmunks scampered among the boulders.

Skye Fargo breathed deep of the pine scent and patted his stallion on the neck. This was his element. He much preferred the open wild places to the wood and brick mazes that passed for cities and towns. Not that he disliked companionship. There were scores of fallen doves scattered throughout the West who could attest to his friendliness.

He stifled a yawn and gazed to the West. He'd been in the saddle since first light, except for two brief stops to give the pinto a rest, and he welcomed the prospect of making camp. Too bad he hadn't thought to borrow some of the robbers' coffee.

The woods thinned out, and by the time the sun hung above the horizon he came to a creek flowing south toward the Snake. Erosion had worn a shallow gully that was perfect for his needs. He rode down the slight slope and reined up. There was plenty of water, shelter from the wind, and no one on the plain above would be able to see them.

Skye swung down and let the stallion drink. He stripped off his saddle, his saddlebags, and the bedroll, then moved aside while the pinto rolled to its heart's delight. Next he took a picket pin, used a rock to pound it into the ground, and tethered the Ovaro in the middle of a lush patch of grass.

The horse attended to, he took care of his own needs. Collecting enough dry wood to last through the night took twenty minutes, and twilight shrouded the landscape when he stretched out on his blankets beside the flickering fire and chewed hungrily on a piece of jerked beef. Tomorrow he planned to treat himself to a hot meal before he got down to business. And a drink or two to wash down the dust from weeks of travel wouldn't hurt either.

Myriad stars blossomed in the heavens and Fargo lay there for almost an hour staring and pondering on how best to go about the job he had to do. Growing thirsty he rose and walked to the creek where he knelt, propped his palms on a flat rock at the water's edge, and drank heartily. Straightening, he wiped his mouth with the back of his sleeve.

The Ovaro nickered.

Fargo stood and turned. He'd ridden the stallion long enough to know the difference between an ordinary neigh and the way it whinnied when it was agitated, and right now it was agitated. A moment later he discovered why.

Slinking down the far side of the gully was one of the largest mountain lions he had ever seen.

Ø **SIGNET** (0451)

# RIDING THE WESTERN TRAIL

☐ THE TRAILSMAN #99: CAMP SAINT LUCIFER by Jon Sharpe. (164431—$3.50)
☐ THE TRAILSMAN #100: RIVERBOAT GOLD by Jon Sharpe. (164814—$3.95)
☐ THE TRAILSMAN #101: SHOSHONI SPIRITS by Jon Sharpe. (165489—$3.50)
☐ THE TRAILSMAN #103: SECRET SIXGUNS by Jon Sharpe. (166116—$3.50)
☐ THE TRAILSMAN #104: COMANCHE CROSSING by Jon Sharpe. (167058—$3.50)
☐ THE TRAILSMAN #105: BLACK HILLS BLOOD by Jon Sharpe. (167260—$3.50)
☐ THE TRAILSMAN #106: SIERRA SHOOT-OUT by Jon Sharpe. (167465—$3.50)
☐ THE TRAILSMAN #107: GUNSMOKE GULCH by Jon Sharpe. (168038—$3.50)
☐ THE TRAILSMAN #108: PAWNEE BARGAIN by Jon Sharpe. (168577—$3.50)
☐ THE TRAILSMAN #109: LONE STAR LIGHTNING by Jon Sharpe. (168801—$3.50)
☐ THE TRAILSMAN #110: COUNTERFEIT CARGO by Jon Sharpe. (168941—$3.50)
☐ THE TRAILSMAN #111: BLOOD CANYON by Jon Sharpe. (169204—$3.50)
☐ THE TRAILSMAN #112: THE DOOMSDAY WAGONS by Jon Sharpe.
(169425—$3.50)
☐ THE TRAILSMAN #113: SOUTHERN BELLES by Jon Sharpe. (169635—$3.50)

Buy them at your local bookstore or use this convenient coupon for ordering.

**NEW AMERICAN LIBRARY**
**P.O. Box 999, Bergenfield, New Jersey 07621**

Please send me the books I have checked above.
I am enclosing $_____ (please add $2.00 to cover postage and handling).
Send check or money order (no cash or C.O.D.'s) or charge by Mastercard or
VISA (with a $15.00 minimum). Prices and numbers are subject to change without
notice.

Card #_____ Exp. Date _____
Signature_____
Name_____
Address_____
City _____ State _____ Zip Code _____

For faster service when ordering by credit card call **1-800-253-6476**

Allow a minimum of 4-6 weeks for delivery. This offer is subject to change without notice.